T0001931

MISTBORN
SECRET
HISTORY

BRANDON SANDERSON

—MISTBORN—
SECRET HISTORY

TOR

A TOM DOHERTY ASSOCIATES BOOK

NEW YORK

This novella contains major spoilers for the original Mistborn trilogy and minor spoilers for *The Bands of Mourning*.

This is a work of fiction. All of the characters, organizations, and events portrayed in this novel are either products of the author's imagination or are used fictitiously.

MISTBORN: SECRET HISTORY

Copyright © 2016 by Dragonsteel Entertainment, LLC

Illustrations copyright © 2016 by Dragonsteel Entertainment, LLC

Brandon Sanderson® and Mistborn® are registered trademarks of Dragonsteel Entertainment, LLC

Marewill symbol by Ben McSweeney © Dragonsteel Entertainment, LLC

All rights reserved.

Illustrations by Ben McSweeney and Isaac Stewart

A Tor Book
Published by Tom Doherty Associates
120 Broadway
New York, NY 10271

www.tor-forge.com

Tor® is a registered trademark of Macmillan Publishing Group, LLC.

The Library of Congress Cataloging-in-Publication Data
is available upon request.

ISBN 978-1-250-85914-3 (paper over board)
ISBN 978-0-7653-9549-8 (ebook)

Our books may be purchased in bulk for promotional, educational, or business use. Please contact your local bookseller or the Macmillan Corporate and Premium Sales Department at 1-800-221-7945, extension 5442, or by email at MacmillanSpecialMarkets@macmillan.com.

First Edition: 2022

Printed in the United States of America

0 9 8 7 6 5 4 3

—MISTBORN—
SECRET HISTORY

PART ONE
EMPIRE

1

Kelsier burned the Eleventh Metal.

Nothing changed. He still stood in that Luthadel square, facing down the Lord Ruler. A hushed audience, both skaa and noble, watched at the perimeter. A squeaking wheel turned lazily in the wind, hanging from the side of the overturned prison wagon nearby. An Inquisitor's head had been nailed to the wood of the wagon's bottom, held in place by its own spikes.

Nothing changed, while everything changed. For to Kelsier's eyes, two men now stood before him.

One was the immortal emperor who had dominated for a thousand years: an imposing figure with jet-black hair and a chest stuck through with two spears that he didn't even seem to notice. Next to him stood a man with the same features—but a completely different demeanor. A figure cloaked in thick furs, nose and cheeks flush as if cold. His hair was tangled and windswept, his attitude jovial, smiling.

It was the same man.

Can I use this? Kelsier thought, frantic.

Black ash fell lightly between them. The Lord Ruler glanced toward the Inquisitor that Kelsier had killed. "Those are very hard to replace," he said, his voice imperious.

That tone seemed a direct contrast to the man beside him: a vagabond, a mountain man wearing the Lord Ruler's face. *This is what you really are,* Kelsier thought. But that didn't help. It was only further proof that the Eleventh Metal wasn't what Kelsier had once hoped. The metal was no magical solution for ending the Lord Ruler. He would have to rely instead upon his other plan.

And so, Kelsier smiled.

"I killed you once," the Lord Ruler said.

"You tried," Kelsier replied, his heart racing. The other plan, the secret plan. "But you can't kill me, Lord Tyrant. I represent that thing you've never been able to kill, no matter how hard you try. I am hope."

The Lord Ruler snorted. He raised a casual arm.

Kelsier braced himself. He could not fight against someone who was immortal.

Not alive, at least.

Stand tall. Give them something to remember.

The Lord Ruler backhanded him. Agony hit Kelsier like a stroke of lightning. In that moment, Kelsier flared the Eleventh Metal, and caught a glimpse of something new.

The Lord Ruler standing in a room—no, a cavern!

The Lord Ruler stepped into a glowing pool and the world shifted around him, rocks crumbling, the room twisting, everything *changing*.

The vision vanished.

Kelsier died.

It turned out to be far more painful a process than he had anticipated. Instead of a soft fade to nothingness, he felt an awful *tearing* sensation—as if he were a cloth caught between the jaws of two vicious hounds.

He screamed, desperately trying to hold himself together. His will meant nothing. He was rent, ripped, and hurled into a place of endless shifting mists.

He stumbled to his knees, gasping, aching. He wasn't certain what he knelt upon, as downward seemed to just be more mist. The ground rippled like liquid, and felt soft to his touch.

He knelt there, enduring, feeling the pain slowly fade away. At last he unclenched his jaw and groaned.

He was alive. Kind of.

He managed to look up. That same thick greyness shifted all around him. A nothingness? No, he could see shapes in it, shadows. Hills? And high in the sky, some kind of light. A tiny sun perhaps, as seen through dense grey clouds.

Kelsier breathed in and out, then growled, heaving himself to his feet. "Well," he proclaimed, "*that* was thoroughly awful."

It did seem there was an afterlife, which was a pleasant discovery. Did this mean . . . did this mean Mare was still out there somewhere? He'd always offered platitudes, talking to the others about being with her again someday. But deep down he'd never believed, never really thought . . .

The end was not the end. Kelsier smiled again, this time truly excited. He turned about, and as he inspected his surroundings, the mists seemed to withdraw. No, it felt like Kelsier was *solidifying,* entering this place fully. The withdrawal of the mists was more like a clearing of his own mind.

The mists coalesced into shapes. Those shadows he'd mistaken for hills were buildings, hazy and formed of shifting mists. The ground beneath his feet was also mist, a deep vastness, like he was standing on the surface of the ocean. It was soft to his touch, like cloth, and even a little springy.

Nearby lay the overturned prison wagon, but here it was made of mist. That mist shifted and moved, but the wagon retained its form. It was like the mist was trapped by some unseen force into a specific shape. More strikingly, the wagon's prison bars *glowed* on this side. Complementing them, other white-hot pinpricks of light appeared around him, dotting the landscape. Doorknobs. Window latches. Everything in the living world was reflected here in this place, and while most things were shadowy mist, metal instead appeared as a powerful light.

Some of those lights moved. He frowned, stepping toward one, and only then did he recognize that many of the lights were people. He saw each as an intense white glow radiating out from a human form.

Metal and souls are the same thing, he observed. Who would have thought?

As he got his bearings, he recognized what was happening in the living world. Thousands of lights moved, flowing away. The crowd was running from the square. A powerful light, with a tall silhouette, strode in another direction. The Lord Ruler.

Kelsier tried to follow, but stumbled over something at his feet. A misty form slumped on the ground, pierced by a spear. Kelsier's own corpse.

Touching it was like remembering a fond experience. Familiar scents from his youth. His mother's voice. The warmth of lying on a hillside with Mare, looking up at the falling ash.

Those experiences faded and seemed to grow *cold.* One of the lights from the mass of fleeing people—it was hard to make out individuals, with everyone alight—scrambled toward him. At first he thought perhaps this person had seen his spirit. But no, they ran to his corpse and knelt.

Now that she was close, he could make out the details of this figure's features, cut of mist and glowing from deep within.

"Ah, child," Kelsier said. "I'm sorry." He reached out and cupped Vin's face as she wept over him, and found he could feel her. She was solid to his ethereal fingers. She didn't seem able to feel his touch, but he caught a vision of her from the real world, cheeks stained with tears.

His last words to her had been harsh, hadn't they? Perhaps it was a good thing that he and Mare had never had children.

A glowing figure surged from the fleeing masses and grabbed Vin. Was that Ham? Had to be, with that profile. Kelsier stood up and watched them withdraw. He had set plans in motion for them. Perhaps they would hate him for that.

"You let him kill you."

Kelsier spun, surprised to find a person standing beside him. Not a figure made of mist, but a man in strange clothing: a thin wool coat that went down almost to his feet, and beneath it a shirt that laced closed, with a kind of conical skirt. That was tied with a belt that had a bone-handled knife stuck through a loop.

The man was short, with black hair and a prominent nose. Unlike the other people—who were made of light—this man looked normal, like Kelsier. Since Kelsier was dead, did this make the man another ghost?

"Who are you?" Kelsier demanded.

"Oh, I think you know." The man met Kelsier's eyes, and in them Kelsier saw eternity. A cool, calm eternity—the eternity of stones that saw generations pass, or of careless depths that didn't notice the changing of days, for light never reached them anyway.

"Oh, hell," Kelsier said. "There's actually a God?"

"Yes."

Kelsier decked him.

It was a good, clean punch, thrown from the shoulder while he brought his other arm up to block a counterstrike. Dox would be proud.

God didn't dodge. Kelsier's punch took him right across the face, connecting with a satisfying *thud*. The punch tossed God to the ground, though when he looked up he seemed more shocked than pained.

Kelsier stepped forward. "What the hell is wrong with you? You're real, and you're letting *this* happen?" He waved toward the square where—to his horror—he saw lights winking out. The Inquisitors were attacking the crowd.

"I do what I can." The fallen figure seemed to distort for a moment, bits of him expanding, like mists escaping an enclosure. "I do . . . I do what I can. It is in motion, you see. I . . ."

Kelsier recoiled a step, eyes widening as God *came apart,* then pulled back together.

Around him, other souls made the transition. Their bodies stopped glowing, then their souls lurched into this land of mists: stumbling, falling, as if ejected from their bodies. Once they arrived, Kelsier saw them in color. The same man—God—appeared near each of them. There were suddenly over a dozen versions of him, each identical, each speaking to one of the dead.

The version of God near Kelsier stood up and rubbed his jaw. "Nobody has ever done that before."

"What, really?" Kelsier asked.

"No. Souls are usually too disoriented. Some do run, though." He looked to Kelsier.

Kelsier made fists. God stepped back and—amusingly—reached for the knife at his belt.

Well, Kelsier wasn't going to attack him, not again. But he *had* heard the challenge in those words. Would he run? Of course not. Where would he run to?

Nearby, an unfortunate skaa woman lurched into the afterlife, then almost immediately *faded*. Her figure stretched, transforming to a white mist that was pulled toward a distant, dark point. That was how it looked, at least, though the point she stretched toward wasn't a place—not really. It was . . . Beyond. A location that was somehow distant, pointing away from him no matter where he moved.

She stretched, then faded away. Other spirits in the square followed.

Kelsier spun on God. "What's happening?"

"You didn't think *this* was the end, did you?" God asked, waving toward the shadowy world. "This is the in-between step. After death and before . . ."

"Before what?"

"Before the Beyond," God said. "The Somewhere Else. Where souls must go. Where *yours* must go."

"I haven't gone yet."

"It takes longer for Allomancers, but it will happen.

It is the natural progress of things, like a stream flowing toward the ocean. I'm here not to make it occur, but to comfort you as you go. I see it as a kind of . . . duty that comes with my position." He rubbed the side of his face and gave Kelsier a glare that said what he thought of his reception.

Nearby, another pair of people faded into the eternities. They seemed to accept it, stepping into the stretching nothingness with relieved, welcoming smiles. Kelsier looked at those departing souls.

"Mare," he whispered.

"She went Beyond. As you will."

Kelsier looked toward that point Beyond, the point toward which all the dead were being drawn. He felt it, faintly, begin to tug on him as well.

No. Not yet.

"We need a plan," Kelsier said.

"A plan?" God asked.

"To get me out of this. I might need your help."

"There *is* no way out of this."

"That's a terrible attitude," Kelsier said. "We'll never get anything done if you talk like that."

He looked at his arm, which was—disconcertingly—starting to blur, like ink on a page that had been accidentally brushed before it dried. He felt a *draining*.

He started walking, forcing himself into a stride. He wouldn't just stand there while eternity tried to suck him away.

"It is natural to feel uncertain," God said, falling

into step beside him. "Many are anxious. Be at peace. The ones you left behind will find their own way, and you—"

"Yes, great," Kelsier said. "No time for lectures. Talk to me. Has anyone ever resisted being pulled into the Beyond?"

"No." God's form pulsed, unraveling again before coming back together. "I've told you already."

Damn, Kelsier thought. *He seems one step from falling apart himself.*

Well, you had to work with what you had. "You've got to have some kind of idea what I could try, Fuzz."

"What did you call me?"

"Fuzz. I've got to call you something."

"You could try 'My Lord,'" Fuzz said with a huff.

"That's a terrible nickname for a crewmember."

"Crewmember . . ."

"I need a team," Kelsier said, still striding through the shadowy version of Luthadel. "And as you can see, my options are limited. I'd rather have Dox, but he's got to go deal with the man who is claiming to be you. Besides, the initiation to this particular team of mine is a killer."

"But—"

Kelsier turned, taking the smaller man by the shoulders. Kelsier's arms were blurring further, drawn away like water being pulled into the current of an invisible stream.

"Look," Kelsier said quietly, urgently, "you said you

were here to comfort me. This is how you do it. If you're right, then nothing I do now will matter. So why not humor me? Let me have one last thrill as I face down the ultimate eventuality."

Fuzz sighed. "It would be better if you accepted what is happening."

Kelsier held Fuzz's gaze. Time was running out; he could *feel* himself sliding toward oblivion, a distant point of nothingness, dark and unknowable. Still he held that gaze. If this creature acted anything like the human he resembled, then holding his eyes—with confidence, smiling, self-assured—would work. Fuzz would bend.

"So," Fuzz said. "You're not only the first to punch me, you're also the first to try to *recruit* me. You are a distinctively strange man."

"You don't know my friends. Next to them I'm normal. Ideas please." He started walking up a street, moving just to be moving. Tenements loomed on either side, made of shifting mists. They looked like the ghosts of buildings. Occasionally a wave—a shimmer of light—would pulse through the ground and buildings, causing the mists to writhe and twist.

"I don't know what you expect me to tell you," Fuzz said, hustling up to walk beside him. "Spirits who come to this place are drawn into the Beyond."

"You aren't."

"I'm a god."

A god. Not just "God." Noted.

"Well," Kelsier said, "what is it about being a god that makes you immune?"

"Everything."

"I can't help thinking you aren't pulling your weight on this team, Fuzz. Come on. Work with me. You indicated that Allomancers last longer. Feruchemists too?"

"Yes."

"People with power," Kelsier said, pointing toward the far-off spires of Kredik Shaw. This was the road the Lord Ruler had taken, heading toward his palace. Though the Lord Ruler's carriage was now distant, Kelsier could still see his soul glowing up there somewhere. Far brighter than the others.

"What about him?" Kelsier said. "You say that everyone has to bend to death, but obviously that isn't true. He is immortal."

"He's a special case," Fuzz said, perking up. "He has ways of not dying in the first place."

"And if he did die?" Kelsier pressed. "He'd last even longer on this side than I am, right?"

"Oh, indeed," Fuzz said. "He Ascended, if just for a short time. He held enough of the power to expand his soul."

Got it. Expand my soul.

"I . . ." God wavered, figure distorting. "I . . ." He cocked his head. "What was I saying?"

"About how the Lord Ruler expanded his soul."

"That was delightful," God said. "It was spectacular to watch! And now he is *Preserved*. I am glad you didn't find a way to destroy him. Everyone else passes, but not him. It's wonderful."

"Wonderful?" Kelsier felt like spitting. "He's a tyrant, Fuzz."

"He's unchanging," God said, defensive. "He's a brilliant specimen. So unique. I don't agree with what he does, but one can empathize with the lamb while admiring the lion, can one not?"

"Why not stop him? If you disagree with what he does, then do something about it!"

"Now, now," God said. "That would be hasty. What would removing him accomplish? It would just raise another leader who is more transient—and cause chaos and even more deaths than the Lord Ruler has caused. Better to have stability. Yes. A constant leader."

Kelsier felt himself stretching further. He'd go soon. It didn't seem his new body could sweat, for if it could have his forehead would certainly be drenched by now.

"Maybe you would enjoy watching another do as he did," Kelsier said. "Expand their soul."

"Impossible. The power at the Well of Ascension won't be gathered and ready for more than a year."

"*What?*" Kelsier said. The *Well of Ascension*?

He dredged through his memories, trying to remember the things Sazed had told him of religion and belief. The scope of it threatened to overwhelm him. He'd been playing at rebellion and thrones—focusing on religion only when he thought it might benefit his plans—and all the while, *this* had been in the background. Ignored and unnoticed.

He felt like a child.

Fuzz kept speaking, oblivious to Kelsier's awakening. "But no, you wouldn't be able to use the Well. I've failed at locking him away. I knew I would; he's stronger. His essence seeps out in natural forms. Solid, liquid, gas. Because of how we created the world. He has plans. But are they deeper than my plans, or have I finally outthought him . . . ?"

Fuzz distorted again. His diatribe made little sense to Kelsier. He felt as if it was important, but it just wasn't *urgent*.

"Power is returning to the Well of Ascension," Kelsier said.

Fuzz hesitated. "Hm. Yes. Um, but it's far, far away. Yes, too far for you to go. Too bad."

God, it turned out, was a terrible liar.

Kelsier seized him, and the little man cringed.

"Tell me," Kelsier said. "Please. I can feel myself stretching away, falling, being pulled. Please."

Fuzz yanked out of his grip. Kelsier's fingers . . . or rather, his soul's fingers . . . weren't working as well any longer.

"No," Fuzz said. "No, it is not right. If you touched it, you might just add to his power. You will go as all others."

Very well, Kelsier thought. *A con, then.*

He let himself slump against the wall of a ghostly building. He sighed, settling down in a seated position, back to the wall. "All right."

"See, there!" Fuzz said. "Better. Much better, isn't it?"

"Yes," Kelsier said.

God seemed to relax. With discomfort, Kelsier noticed God was still leaking. Mist slipped away from his body at a few pinprick points. This creature was like a wounded beast, placidly going about its daily life while ignoring the bite marks.

Remaining motionless was hard. Harder than facing down the Lord Ruler had been. Kelsier wanted to run, to scream, to scramble and move. That sensation of being drawn away was *horrible.*

Somehow he feigned relaxation. "You asked," he said, as if very tired and having trouble forcing it out, "me a question? When you first appeared?"

"Oh!" Fuzz said. "Yes. You let him kill you. I had not expected that."

"You're God. Can't you see the future?"

"To an extent," Fuzz said, animated. "But it is cloudy, so cloudy. Too many possibilities. I did not see this among them, though it was probably there. You must tell me. Why *did* you let him kill you? At the end, you just stood there."

"I couldn't have gotten away," Kelsier said. "Once the Lord Ruler arrived, there was no escaping. I had to confront him."

"You didn't even fight."

"I used the Eleventh Metal."

"Foolishness," God said. He started pacing. "That was Ruin's influence on you. But what was the point? I can't understand why he wanted you to have that useless metal." He perked up. "And that *fight*. You and the Inquisitor. Yes, I've seen many things, but that was unlike any other. Impressive, though I wish you hadn't caused such destruction, Kelsier."

He continued pacing, but seemed to have more of a spring to his step. Kelsier hadn't expected God to be so . . . human. Excitable, even energetic.

"I saw something," Kelsier said, "as the Lord Ruler killed me. The person as he might once have been. His past? A version of his past? He stood at the Well of Ascension."

"Did you? Hmm. Yes, the metal, flared during the moment of transition. You got a glimpse of the Spiritual Realm, then? His Connection and his past? You were using Ati's essence, unfortunately. One shouldn't trust it, even in a diluted form. Except . . ." He frowned, cocking his head, as if trying to remember something he'd forgotten.

"Another god," Kelsier whispered, closing his eyes. "You said . . . you trapped him?"

"He will break free eventually. It's inevitable. But the prison isn't my last gambit. It can't be."

Perhaps I should just let go, Kelsier thought, drifting.

"There now," God said. "Farewell, Kelsier. You served *him* more often than you did me, but I can respect your intentions, *and* your remarkable ability to Preserve yourself."

"I saw it," Kelsier whispered. "A cavern high in the mountains. The Well of Ascension . . ."

"Yes," Fuzz said. "That's where I put it."

"But . . ." Kelsier said, stretching, "he moved it. . . ."

"Naturally."

What would the Lord Ruler do, with a source of such power? Hide it far away?

Or keep it very, very close? Near to his fingertips. Hadn't Kelsier seen furs, like the ones he'd seen the Lord Ruler wearing in his vision? He'd seen them in a room, past an Inquisitor. A building within a building, hidden within the depths of the palace.

Kelsier opened his eyes.

Fuzz spun toward him. "What—"

Kelsier heaved himself to his feet and started running. There wasn't much *self* to him left, just a fuzzy blurred image. The feet that he ran upon were distorted smudges, his form a pulled-out, unraveling piece of cloth. He barely found purchase upon the misty ground, and when he stumbled against a building, he *pushed* through it, ignoring the wall as one might a stiff breeze.

"So you *are* a runner," Fuzz said, appearing beside him. "Kelsier, child, this accomplishes nothing. I suppose I should have expected nothing less from you. Frantically butting against your destiny until the last moment."

Kelsier barely heard the words. He focused on the run, on resisting that grip *hauling* him backward, into the nothing. He raced the grip of death itself, its cold fingers closing around him.

Run.

Concentrate.

Struggle to *be*.

The flight reminded him of another time, climbing through a pit, arms bloodied. He would *not be taken*!

The pulsing became his guide, that wave that washed periodically through the shadowy world. He sought its source. He barreled through buildings, crossed thoroughfares, ignoring both metal and the souls of men until he reached the grey mist silhouette of Kredik Shaw, the Hill of a Thousand Spires.

Here, Fuzz seemed to grasp what was going on.

"You zinc-tongued raven," the god said, moving beside him without effort while Kelsier ran with everything he had. "You're not going to reach it in time."

He was running through mists again. Walls, people, buildings faded. Nothing but dark, swirling mists.

But the mists had never been his enemy.

With the thumping of those pulses to guide him, Kelsier strained through the swirling nothingness until a pillar of light exploded before him. It was there! He could see it, burning in the mists. He could almost touch it, almost . . .

He was losing it. Losing himself. He could move no more.

Something seized him.

"Please . . ." Kelsier whispered, falling, sliding away.

This is not right. Fuzz's voice.

"You want to see something . . . spectacular?" Kelsier whispered. "Help me live. I'll *show* you . . . *spectacular.*"

Fuzz wavered, and Kelsier could sense the divinity's hesitance. It was followed by a sense of purpose, like a lamp being lit, and laughter.

Very well. Be Preserved, Kelsier. Survivor.

Something shoved him forward, and Kelsier merged with the light.

Moments later he blinked awake. He lay in the misty world still, but his body—or, well, his spirit—had reformed. He lay in a pool of light like liquid metal. He could feel its warmth all around him, invigorating.

He could make out a misty cavern outside the pool; it seemed to be made of natural rock, though he couldn't tell for certain, because it was all mist on this side.

The pulsing surged through him.

"The power," Fuzz said, standing beyond the light. "You are now part of it, Kelsier."

"Yeah," Kelsier said, climbing to his feet, dripping with radiant light. "I can feel it, thrumming through me."

"You are trapped with him," Fuzz said. He seemed shallow, wan, compared to the powerful light that Kelsier stood amid. "I warned you. This is a prison."

Kelsier settled down, breathing in and out. "I'm alive."

"According to a very loose definition of the word."

Kelsier smiled. "It'll do."

Immortality proved to be far more frustrating than Kelsier had anticipated.

Of course, he didn't know if he was *truly* immortal or not. He didn't have a heartbeat—which was only unnerving when he noticed it—and didn't need to breathe. But who could say if his soul aged or not in this place?

In the hours following his survival, Kelsier inspected his new home. God was right, it *was* a prison. The pool he was in grew deep at the center point, and was filled with liquid light that seemed a reflection of something more . . . potent on the other side.

Fortunately, though the Well was not wide, only the very center was deeper than he was tall. He could stay around the perimeter and only be in the light up to his waist. It was thin, thinner than water, and easy to move through.

He could also step out of this pool and its attached pillar of light, settling onto the rocky side. Everything in this cavern was made of mist, though the edges of the Well . . . He seemed to see the stone better here, more fully. It appeared to have some actual color to it. As if this place were part spirit, like him.

He could sit on the edge of the Well, legs dangling into the light. But if he tried to walk too far from the Well, misty wisps of that same power trailed him and held him back, like chains. They wouldn't let him get more than a few feet from the pool. He tried straining, pushing, dashing and throwing himself out, but nothing worked. He always pulled up sharply once he got a few feet away.

After several hours of trying to break free, Kelsier slumped on the side of the Well, feeling . . . exhausted? Was that even the right word? He had no body, and felt no traditional signs of tiredness. No headache, no strained muscles. But he *was* fatigued. Worn out like an old banner allowed to flap in the wind through too many rainstorms.

Forced to relax, he took stock of what little he could make out of his surroundings. Fuzz was gone; the god had been distracted by something a short time after Kelsier's Preservation, and had vanished. That left Kelsier with a cavern made of shadows, the glowing pool itself, and some pillars extending through the chamber. At the other end, he saw the glow of bits of metal, though he couldn't figure out what they were.

This was the sum of his existence. Had he just locked himself away in this little prison for eternity?

It seemed an ultimate irony to him that he might have managed to cheat death, only to find himself suffering a fate far worse.

What would happen to his mind if he spent a few decades in here? A few *centuries*?

He sat on the rim of the Well, and tried to distract himself by thinking about his friends. He'd trusted in his plans at the moment of his death, but now he saw so many holes in his plot to inspire a rebellion. What if the skaa didn't rise up? What if the stockpiles he'd prepared weren't enough?

Even if that all worked, so much would ride upon the shoulders of some very ill-prepared men. And one remarkable young woman.

Lights drew his attention, and he leaped to his feet, eager for any distraction. A group of figures, outlined as glowing souls, had entered this room in the world of the living. There was something odd about them. Their eyes . . .

Inquisitors.

Kelsier refused to flinch, though by every instinct he dreaded these creatures. He had bested one of their champions. He would fear them no longer. Instead, he paced his confines, trying to discern what the three Inquisitors were lugging toward him. Something large and heavy, but it didn't glow at all.

A body, Kelsier realized. *Headless.*

Was this the one he'd killed? Yes, it must be. Another Inquisitor was reverently carrying the dead one's spikes, a whole pile of them, all placed together inside a large jar of liquid. Kelsier squinted at it, taking a single step out of his prison, trying to determine what he was seeing.

"Blood," Fuzz said, suddenly standing nearby. "They store the spikes in blood until they can be used again. In that way, they can prevent the spikes from losing their effectiveness."

"Huh," Kelsier said, stepping to the side as the Inquisitors tossed the body into the Well, then dropped in the head. Both evaporated. "Do they do this often?"

"Each time one of their number dies," Fuzz said. "I doubt they even know what they are doing. Tossing a dead body into that pool is beyond meaningless."

The Inquisitors retreated with the spikes of the fallen. Judging by their slumped forms, the four creatures were exhausted.

"My plan," Kelsier said, looking to Fuzz. "How is it going? My crew should have discovered the warehouse by now. The people of the city . . . did it work? Are the skaa angry?"

"Hmmm?" Fuzz asked.

"The revolution, the plan," Kelsier said, stepping toward him. God shifted backward, getting just beyond where Kelsier would be able to reach, hand going to the knife at his belt. Perhaps that punch earlier had been ill-advised. "Fuzz, listen. You have to go nudge them. We'll never have a better chance of overthrowing him."

"The plan . . ." Fuzz said. He unraveled for a moment, before returning. "Yes, there was a plan. I . . . remember I had a plan. When I was smarter . . ."

"The plan," Kelsier said, "is to get the skaa to revolt. It won't matter how powerful the Lord Ruler is, won't matter if he's immortal, once we toss him in chains and lock him away."

Fuzz nodded, distracted.

"Fuzz?"

He shook, glancing toward Kelsier, and the sides of his head unraveled slowly—like a fraying rug, each thread seeping away and vanishing into nothing. "He's killing me, you know. He wants me gone before the next cycle, though . . . perhaps I can hold out. You hear me, Ruin! I'm not dead yet. Still . . . still here . . ."

Hell, Kelsier thought, cold. *God is going insane.*

Fuzz started pacing. "I know you're listening, changing what I write, what I have written. You make our religion all about you. They hardly remember the truth any longer. Subtle as always, you worm."

"Fuzz," Kelsier said. "Could you just go—"

"I needed a sign," Fuzz whispered, stopping near Kelsier. "Something he couldn't change. A sign of the weapon I'd buried. The boiling point of water, I think. Maybe its freezing point? But what if the units change over the years? I needed something that would be remembered always. Something they'll immediately recognize." He leaned in. "Sixteen."

"Six . . . teen?" Kelsier said.

"Sixteen." Fuzz grinned. "Clever, don't you think?"

"Because it means . . ."

"The number of metals," Fuzz said. "In Allomancy."

"There are ten. Eleven, if you count the one I discovered."

"No! No, no, that's stupid. Sixteen. It's the perfect number. They'll see. They have to see." Fuzz started pacing again, and his head returned—mostly—to its earlier state.

Kelsier sat down on the rim of his prison. God's actions were far more erratic than they had been earlier. Had something changed, or—like a human with a mental disease—was God simply better at some times than he was at others?

Fuzz looked up abruptly. He winced, turning his eyes toward the ceiling, as if it were going to collapse on him. He opened his mouth, jaw working, but made no sound.

"What . . ." he finally said. "What have you *done*?"

Kelsier stood up in his prison.

"What have you done?" Fuzz screamed.

Kelsier smiled. "Hope," he said softly. "I have hoped."

"He was perfect," Fuzz said. "He was . . . the only one of you . . . that . . ." He spun suddenly, gazing down the shadowy room beyond Kelsier's prison.

Someone stood at the other end. A tall, commanding figure, not made of light. Familiar clothing, of both white and black, contrasting with itself.

The Lord Ruler. His spirit, at least.

Kelsier stepped up onto the rim of stone around the pool and waited as the Lord Ruler strode toward the light of the Well. He stopped in place when he noticed Kelsier.

"I killed you," the Lord Ruler said. "Twice. Yet you live."

"Yes. We're all aware of how strikingly incompetent you are. I'm glad you're beginning to see it for yourself. That's the first step toward change."

The Lord Ruler sniffed and looked around at the chamber, with its diaphanous walls. His eyes passed over Fuzz, but he didn't give the god much consideration.

Kelsier exulted. She'd done it. She'd actually *done it*. How? What secret had he missed?

"That grin," the Lord Ruler said to Kelsier, "is insufferable. I *did* kill you."

"I returned the favor."

"You *didn't* kill me, Survivor."

"I forged the blade that did."

Fuzz cleared his throat. "It is my duty to be with you as you transition. Don't be worried, or—"

"Be silent," the Lord Ruler said, inspecting Kelsier's prison. "Do you know what you've done, Survivor?"

"I've won."

"You've brought Ruin upon the world. You are a pawn. So proud, like a soldier on the battlefield, confident he controls his own destiny—while ignoring the thousands upon thousands in his rank." He shook his head. "Only a year left. So close. I would have again ransomed this undeserving planet."

"This is just . . ." Fuzz swallowed. "This is an in-between step. After death and before the Some-where Else. Where souls must go. Where *yours* must go, Rashek."

Rashek? Kelsier looked again at the Lord Ruler. You could not tell a Terrisman by skin tone; that was a mistake many people made. Some Terris were dark, others light. Still, he would have thought . . .

The room filled with furs. This man, in the cold.

Idiot. That was what it meant, of course.

"It was all a lie," Kelsier said. "A trick. Your fabled immortality? Your healing? Feruchemy. But how did you become an Allomancer?"

The Lord Ruler stepped right up to the pillar of light that rose from the prison, and the two stared at one another. As they had on that square above when alive.

Then the Lord Ruler stuck his hand into the light.

Kelsier set his jaw and pictured sudden, horrify-ing images of spending an eternity trapped with the man who had murdered Mare. The Lord Ruler pulled his hand out, however, trailing light like molasses. He turned his hand over, inspecting the glow, which eventually faded.

"So now what?" Kelsier asked. "You remain here?"

"Here?" The Lord Ruler laughed. "With an impo-tent mouse and a half-blooded rat? Please."

He closed his eyes, and then he stretched toward

that point that defied geometry. He faded, then finally vanished.

Kelsier gaped. "He *left*?"

"To the Somewhere Else," Fuzz said, sitting down. "I should not have been so hopeful. Everything passes, nothing is eternal. That is what Ati always claimed. . . ."

"He didn't have to leave," Kelsier said. "He could have remained. Could have survived!"

"I told you, by this point rational people *want* to move on." Fuzz vanished.

Kelsier remained standing there, at the edge of his prison, the glowing pool tossing his shadow across the floor. He stared into the misty room with its columns, waiting for something, though he wasn't certain what. Confirmation, celebration, a change of some sort.

Nothing. Nobody came, not even the Inquisitors. How had the revolution gone? Were the skaa now rulers of society? He would have liked to see the deaths of the noble ranks, treated—in turn—as they had treated their slaves.

He received no confirmation, no sign, of what was happening above. They didn't know about the Well, obviously. All Kelsier could do was settle down.

And wait.

PART TWO
WELL

1

What Kelsier would have given for a pencil and paper.

Something to write on, some way to pass the time. A means of collecting his thoughts and creating a plan of escape.

As the days passed, he tried scratching notes into the sides of the Well, which proved impossible. He tried unraveling threads from his clothing, then tying knots in them to represent words. Unfortunately, threads vanished soon after he pulled them free, and his shirt and trousers immediately returned to the way they'd looked before. Fuzz, during one of his rare visits, explained that the clothing wasn't real—or rather, it was just an extension of Kelsier's spirit.

For the same reason, he couldn't use his hair or blood to write. He didn't technically have either. It was supremely frustrating, but sometime during his second month of imprisonment he admitted the truth to himself. Writing wasn't all that important. He'd never been able to write while confined to the Pits, but he'd planned all the same. Yes, they had been feverish plans, impossible dreams, but lack of paper hadn't stopped him.

The attempts to write weren't about making plans so much as finding something to do. A quest to soak up his time. It had worked for a few weeks. But in acknowledging the truth, he lost his will to keep trying to find a way to write.

Fortunately, about the time he acknowledged this, he discovered something new about his prison.

Whispering.

Oh, he couldn't *hear* it. But could he "hear" anything? He didn't have ears. He was . . . what had Fuzz said? A Cognitive Shadow? A force of mind, holding his spirit together, preventing it from diffusing. Saze would have had a field day. He loved mystical topics like this.

Regardless, Kelsier *could* sense something. The Well continued to pulse as it had before, sending waves of writhing shock through the walls of his prison and out into the world. Those pulses seemed to be strengthening, a continuous thrumming, like the sense bronze lent one in "hearing" people using Allomancy.

Inside of each pulse was . . . something. Whispers, he called them—though they contained more than just words. They were saturated with sounds, scents, and images.

He saw a book, with ink staining its pages. A group of people sharing a story. Terrismen in robes? Sazed?

The pulses whispered chilling words. *Hero of Ages. The Announcer. Worldbringer.* He recognized those terms from the ancient Terris prophecies mentioned in Alendi's logbook.

Kelsier knew the discomforting truth now. He had *met* a god, which meant there was real depth and reality to faith. Did this mean there was something to that array of religions Saze had kept in his pocket, like playing cards to stack a deck?

You have brought Ruin upon this world....

Kelsier settled into the powerful light that was the Well, and found—with practice—that if he submerged himself in the center right before a pulse, he could ride it a short distance. It sent his consciousness traveling out of the Well to catch glimpses of each pulse's destination.

He thought he saw libraries, quiet chambers where distant Terrismen spoke, exchanging stories and memorizing them. He saw madmen huddled in streets, whispering the words the pulses delivered. He saw a Mistborn man, noble, jumping between buildings.

Something other than Kelsier rode with those pulses. Something directing an unseen work, something interested in the lore of the Terris. It took Kelsier an embarrassingly long time to realize he should try another tack. He dunked himself into the center of the pool, surrounded by the too-thin liquid light, and when the next pulse came he pushed himself in the opposite direction—not along with the pulse, but toward its source.

The light thinned, and he looked into someplace new. A dark expanse that was neither the world of the dead nor the world of the living.

In that other place, he found *destruction*.

Decay. Not blackness, for blackness was too complete, too *whole* to represent this thing he sensed in the Beyond. It was a vast force that would gleefully take something as simple as darkness, then rip it apart.

This force was time infinite. It was the winds that weathered, the storms that broke, the timeless waves running slowly, slowly, slowly to a stop as the sun and the planet cooled to nothing.

It was the ultimate end and destiny of all things. And it was angry.

Kelsier pulled back, throwing himself up out of the light, gasping, trembling.

He had met God. But for every Push, there was a Pull. What was the opposite of God?

What he had seen troubled him so much that he almost didn't return. He almost convinced himself to ignore the terrible thing in the darkness. He nearly blocked out the whispers and tried to pretend he had never seen that awesome, vast destroyer.

But of course he couldn't do that. Kelsier had never been able to resist a secret. This thing, even more than meeting Fuzz, proved that Kelsier had been playing all along at a game whose rules far outmatched his understanding.

That both terrified and excited him.

And so, he returned to gaze upon the thing. Again and again he went, struggling to comprehend, though he felt like an ant trying to understand a symphony.

He did this for weeks, right up until the point when the thing *looked* at him.

Before, it hadn't seemed to notice—as one might not notice the spider hiding inside a keyhole. This time though, Kelsier somehow alerted it. The thing churned in an abrupt change of motion, then *flowed* toward Kelsier, its essence surrounding the place from which Kelsier observed. It rotated slowly about itself in a vortex—like an ocean that began turning around one spot. Kelsier couldn't help but feel that an infinite, vast eye was suddenly *squinting* at him.

He fled, splashing, kicking up the liquid light as he backed away into his prison. He was so alarmed that he felt a phantom *heartbeat* thrumming inside of him, his essence acknowledging the proper reaction to shock and trying to replicate it. That stilled as he settled into his customary seat at the side of the pool.

The sight of that thing turning its attention upon him, the sensation of being tiny in the face of something so vast, deeply troubled Kelsier. For all his confidence and plotting, he was basically nothing. His

entire life had been an exercise in unintentional bra-
vado.

Months passed. He didn't return to study the thing
Beyond; Kelsier instead waited for Fuzz to visit and
check in on him, as he did periodically.

When Fuzz finally arrived, he looked even more
unraveled than the last time, mists escaping from his
shoulders, a small hole in his left cheek exposing a
view into his mouth, his clothing growing ragged.

"Fuzz?" Kelsier asked. "I saw something. This . . .
Ruin you spoke of. I think I can watch it."

Fuzz just paced back and forth, not even speaking.

"Fuzz? Hey, are you listening?"

Nothing.

"Idiot," Kelsier tried. "Hey, you're a disgrace to
deityhood. Are you paying attention?"

Even an insult didn't work. Fuzz just kept pacing.

Useless, Kelsier thought as a pulse of power left the
Well. He happened to catch a glimpse of Fuzz's eyes
as the pulse passed.

And in that moment, Kelsier was reminded why he
had named this creature a god in the first place. There
was an infinity beyond those eyes, a complement to
the one trapped here in this Well. Fuzz was the infinity
of a note held perfectly, never wavering. The majesty of
a painting, frozen and still, capturing a slice of life from
a time gone by. It was the power of many, many moments compressed somehow into one.

Fuzz stopped before him and his cheeks unraveled

fully, revealing a skeleton beneath that was also unraveling, eyes glowing with eternity. This creature *was* a divinity; he was just a broken one.

Fuzz left, and Kelsier didn't see him for many months. The stillness and silence of his prison seemed as endless as the creatures he had studied. At one point, he found himself planning how to draw the attention of the destructive one, if only to beg it to end him.

It was when he started talking to himself that he really got worried.

"What have you done?"

"I've saved the world. Freed mankind."

"Gotten revenge."

"The goals can align."

"You are a coward."

"I changed the world!"

"And if you're just a pawn of that thing Beyond? Like the Lord Ruler claimed? Kelsier, what if you have no destiny other than to do as you're told?"

He contained the outburst, recovered himself, but the fragility of his own sanity unnerved him. He hadn't been completely sane in the Pits either. In a moment of stillness—staring at the shifting mists that made up the walls of the cavernous room—he admitted a deeper secret to himself.

He hadn't been completely sane *since* the Pits.

That was one reason why he didn't at first trust his senses when someone spoke to him.

"Now *this* I did not expect."

Kelsier shook himself, then turned with suspicion, worried he was hallucinating. It was possible to see all kinds of things in those shifting mists that made up the walls of the cavern, if you stared at them long enough.

This, however, was not a figure made of mist. It was a man with stark white hair, his face defined by angular features and a sharp nose. He seemed vaguely familiar to Kelsier, but he couldn't place why.

The man sat on the floor, one leg up and his arm resting upon his knee. In his hand he held some kind of stick.

Wait . . . no, he wasn't sitting on the floor, but on an object that somehow seemed to be *floating* upon the mists. The white, loglike object sank halfway into the mists of the floor and rocked like a ship on the water, bobbing in place. The rod in the man's hand was a short oar, and his other leg—the one that wasn't up— rested over the side of the log and vanished into the misty ground, visible only as an obscured silhouette.

"You," the man said to Kelsier, "are very bad at doing as you're supposed to."

"Who are you?" Kelsier asked, stepping to the edge of his prison, eyes narrowed. This was no hallucination. He refused to believe his sanity was that far gone. "A spirit?"

"Alas," the man said, "death has never really suited

me. Bad for the complexion, you see." He studied Kelsier, lips raised in a knowing smile.

Kelsier hated him immediately.

"Got stuck there, did you?" the man said. "In Ati's prison . . ." He clicked his tongue. "Fitting recompense, for what you did. Poetic even."

"What I did?"

"Destroying the Pits, O scarred one. That was the only perpendicularity on this planet with any reasonable ease of access. This one is *very* dangerous, growing more so by the minute, and difficult to find. By doing as you did, you basically ended traffic through Scadrial. Upended an entire mercantile ecosystem, which I'll admit was fun to watch."

"Who *are* you?" Kelsier said.

"I?" the man said. "I am a drifter. A miscreant. The flame's last breath, made of smoke at its passing."

"That's . . . needlessly obtuse."

"Well, I'm that too." The man cocked his head. "That mostly, if I'm honest."

"And you claim to *not* be dead?"

"If I were, would I need this?" the Drifter said, knocking his oar against the front of his small log-like vessel. It bobbed at the motion, and for the first time Kelsier was able to make out what it was. Arms he'd missed before, hanging down into the mists, obscured. A head that drooped on its neck. A white robe, masking the shape.

"A corpse," he whispered.

"Oh, Spanky here is just a spirit. It's damnably difficult to get about in this subastral—anyone physical risks slipping through these mists and falling, perhaps forever. So many thoughts pool together here, becoming what you see around you, and you need something finer to travel over it all."

"That's horrible."

"Says the man who built a revolution upon the backs of the dead. At least I only need *one* corpse."

Kelsier folded his arms. This man was wary—though he spoke lightheartedly, he watched Kelsier with care, and held back as if contemplating a method of attack.

He wants something, Kelsier guessed. *Something that I have, maybe?* No, he seemed legitimately surprised that Kelsier was there. He had come here, intending to visit the Well. Perhaps he wanted to enter it, access the power? Or did he, perhaps, just want to have a look at the thing Beyond?

"Well, you're obviously resourceful," Kelsier said. "Perhaps you can help me with my predicament."

"Alas," the Drifter said. "Your case is hopeless."

Kelsier felt his heart sink.

"Yes, nothing to be done," the Drifter continued. "You are, indeed, stuck with that face. By manifesting those same features on this side, you show that even your *soul* is resigned to you always looking like one ugly sonofa—"

"Bastard," Kelsier cut in. "You had me for a second."

"Now, that's demonstrably wrong," the Drifter said, pointing. "I believe only one of us in this room is illegitimate, and it isn't me. Unless . . ." He tapped the floating corpse on the head with his oar. "What about you, Spanky?"

The corpse actually mumbled something.

"Happily married parents? Still alive? Really? I'm sorry for their loss." The Drifter looked to Kelsier, smiling innocently. "No bastards on this side. What about yours?"

"The bastard by birth," Kelsier said, "is always better off than the one by choice, Drifter. I'll own up to my nature if you own up to yours."

The Drifter chuckled, eyes alight. "Nice, nice. Tell me, since we're on the topic, which are you? A skaa with noble bearing, or a nobleman with skaa interests? Which half is more *you*, Survivor?"

"Well," Kelsier said dryly, "considering that the relatives of my noble half spent the better part of four decades trying to exterminate me, I'd say I'm more inclined toward the skaa side."

"Aaaah," the Drifter said, leaning forward. "But I didn't ask which you liked more. I asked which you *were*."

"Is it relevant?"

"It's *interesting*," the Drifter said. "Which is enough for me." He reached down to the corpse he was using as a boat, then removed something from his pocket. Something that glowed, though Kelsier couldn't tell if it was something naturally radiant, or just something made of metal.

The glow faded as the Drifter administered it to his vessel, then—covering the motion with a cough, as if to hide from Kelsier what he was doing—furtively applied some of the glow to his oar. When he placed the oar back into the mists, it sent the boat scooting closer to the Well.

"*Is* there a way for me to escape this prison?" Kelsier asked.

"How about this?" the Drifter said. "We'll have an insult battle. Winner gets to ask one question, and the other has to answer truthfully. I'll start. What's wet, ugly, and has scars on its arms?"

Kelsier raised an eyebrow. All of this talk was a distraction, as evidenced by Drifter scooting—again—closer to the prison. *He's going to try to jump for the Well,* Kelsier thought. *Leap in, hoping to be fast enough to surprise me.*

"No guess?" Drifter asked. "The answer is basically anyone who spends time with you, Kelsier, as they end up slitting their wrists, hitting themselves in the face, and then drowning themselves to forget the experience. Ha! Okay, your turn."

"I'm going to murder you," Kelsier said softly.

"I— Wait, *what*?"

"If you step inside here," Kelsier said, "I'm going to

murder you. I'll slice the tendons on your wrists so your hands can't do anything more than batter at me uselessly as I kneel against your throat and slowly crush the life out of you—all while I remove your fingers one by one. I'll finally let you breathe a single, frantic gasp—but at that moment I'll shove your middle finger between your lips so that you're forced to suck it down as you struggle for air. You'll go out knowing you choked to death on your own rotten flesh."

The Drifter gaped at him, mouth working soundlessly. "I . . ." he finally said. "I don't think you know how to play this game."

Kelsier shrugged.

"Seriously," Drifter said. "You need some help, friend. I know a guy. Tall, bald, wears lots of earrings. Have a chat with him next—"

The Drifter cut off midsentence and leaped for the prison, kicking off the floating corpse and throwing himself at the light.

Kelsier was ready. As Drifter entered the light, Kelsier grabbed the man by one arm and slung him toward the side of the pool. The maneuver worked, and Drifter seemed to be able to touch the walls and floor here in the Well. He slammed against the wall, sending waves of light splashing up.

As Kelsier tried to punch at Drifter's head while he was stumbling, the man caught himself on the side of the pool and kicked backward, knocking Kelsier's legs out from beneath him.

Kelsier splashed in the light, and he tried to burn metals by reflex. Nothing happened, though there was *something* to the light here. Something familiar—

He managed to get to his feet, and caught Drifter lunging for the center, the deepest part. Kelsier snatched the man by the arm, swinging him away. Whatever this man wanted, Kelsier's instincts said that he shouldn't be allowed to have it. Beyond that, the Well was Kelsier's only asset. If he could hold the man back from what he wanted, subdue him, perhaps it would lead to answers.

The Drifter stumbled, then lunged, trying to grab Kelsier.

Kelsier, in turn, pivoted and buried his fist in the man's stomach. The motion gave him a thrill; after sitting for so long, inactive, it was nice to be able to *do* something.

Drifter grunted at the punch. "All right then," he muttered.

Kelsier brought his fists up, checked his footing, then unleashed a series of quick blows at Drifter's face that *should* have dazed him.

When Kelsier pulled back—not wanting to go too far and hurt the man seriously—he found that Drifter was smiling at him.

That didn't seem a good sign.

Somehow, Drifter shook off the hits he'd taken. He jumped forward, dodged Kelsier's attempted punch, then ducked and *slammed* his fist into Kelsier's kidneys.

It *hurt*. Kelsier lacked a body, but apparently his spirit could feel pain. He let out a grunt and brought up his arms to protect his face, stepping backward in the liquid light. The Drifter attacked, relentless, slamming his fists into Kelsier with no care for the damage he might be doing to himself.

Go to the ground, Kelsier's instincts told him. He dropped one hand and tried to seize Drifter by the arm, planning to send them both down into the light to grapple.

Unfortunately, the Drifter was a little too quick. He dodged and kicked Kelsier's legs from beneath him again, then grabbed him by the throat, slamming him repeatedly—brutally—against the bottom of the shallower part of the prison, splashing him in light that was too thin to be water, but suffocating nonetheless.

Finally Drifter hauled him up, limp. The man's eyes were glowing. "That was unpleasant," Drifter said, "yet somehow still satisfying. Apparently you already being dead means I can hurt you." As Kelsier tried to grab his arm, Drifter slammed Kelsier down again, then pulled him back up, stunned.

"I'm sorry, Survivor, for the rough treatment," Drifter continued. "But you are *not* supposed to be here. You did what I needed you to, but you're a wild card I'd rather not deal with right now." He paused. "If it's any consolation, you should feel proud. It's been centuries since anyone got the drop on me."

He released Kelsier, letting him slump down and catch himself against the side of the prison, half submerged in the light. He growled, trying to pull himself up after Drifter.

Drifter sighed, then proceeded to *kick* at Kelsier's leg repeatedly, shocking him with the pain of it. He screamed, holding his leg. It should have cracked from the force of those kicks, and though it had not, the pain was overwhelming.

"This is a lesson," Drifter said, though it was difficult to hear the words through the pain. "But not the one you might think it is. You don't have a body, and I don't have the inclination to actually injure your soul. That pain is caused by your mind; it's thinking about what *should* be happening to you, and responding." He hesitated. "I'll refrain from making you choke on a chunk of your own flesh."

He walked toward the middle of the pool. Kelsier watched through eyes quivering with pain as Drifter held his hands out to the sides and closed his eyes. He stepped into the center of the pool, the deep portion, and vanished into the light.

A moment later, a figure climbed back out of the pool. Yet this time, the person was shadowy, glowing with inner light like . . .

Like someone in the world of the living. This pool

had let Drifter transition from the world of the dead to the real world. Kelsier gaped, following Drifter with his eyes as the man strode past the pillars in the room, then stopped at the other side. Two tiny sources of metal still glowed fiercely there to Kelsier's eyes.

Drifter selected one. It was small, as he could toss it into the air and catch it again. Kelsier could sense the triumph in that motion.

Kelsier closed his eyes and concentrated. No pain. His leg wasn't actually hurt. *Concentrate.*

He managed to make some of the pain fade. He sat up in the pool, rippling light coming up to his chest. He breathed in and out, though he didn't need the air.

Damn. The first person he'd seen in months had thrashed him, then stolen something from the chamber outside. He didn't know what, or why, or even how the Drifter had managed to slip from one world to the next.

Kelsier crawled to the center of the pool, lowering himself down into the deep portion. He stood, his leg still aching faintly, and put his hands to the sides. He concentrated, trying to . . .

To what? Transition? What would that even do to him?

He didn't care. He was frustrated and humiliated. He needed to prove to himself that he wasn't incapable.

He failed. No amount of concentration, visualization, or straining of muscles made him do what the

Drifter had managed. He climbed from the pool, exhausted and chastened, and settled on the side.

He didn't notice Fuzz standing there until the god spoke. "What were you *doing*?"

Kelsier turned. Fuzz visited infrequently these days, but when he did come, he always did it unannounced. If he spoke, he often only raved like a madman.

"Someone was just here," Kelsier said. "A man with white hair. He somehow used this Well to pass from the world of the dead to the world of the living."

"I see," Fuzz said softly. "He dared that, did he? Dangerous, with Ruin straining against his bonds. But if anyone were going to try something so foolhardy, it would be Cephandrius."

"He stole something, I think," Kelsier said. "From the other side of the room. A bit of metal."

"Aaah . . ." Fuzz said softly. "I had thought that when he rejected the rest of us, he would stop interfering. I should know better than to trust an implication from him. Half the time you can't trust his outright promises. . . ."

"Who is he?" Kelsier asked.

"An old friend. And no, before you ask, you can't do as he did and transition between Realms. Your ties to the Physical Realm have been severed. You're a kite with no string connecting it to the ground. You cannot ride the perpendicularity across."

Kelsier sighed. "Then why was he able to come to the world of the dead?"

"It's not the world of the dead. It's the world of the mind. Men—all things, truly—are like a ray of light. The floor is the Physical Realm, where that light pools. The sun is the Spiritual Realm, where it begins. This Realm, the Cognitive Realm, is the space between where that beam stretches."

The metaphor barely made any sense to him. *They all know so much,* Kelsier thought, *and I know so little.*

Still, at least Fuzz was sounding better today. Kelsier smiled toward the god, then froze as Fuzz turned his head.

Fuzz was missing half his face. The entire left side was just gone. Not wounded, and there was no skeleton. The complete half smoked, trailing wisps of mist. Half his lips remained, and he smiled back at Kelsier, as if nothing were wrong.

"He stole a bit of my essence, distilled and pure," Fuzz explained. "It can Invest a human, grant him or her Allomancy."

"Your . . . face, Fuzz . . ."

"Ati thinks to finish me," Fuzz said. "Indeed, his knife was placed long ago. I'm already dead." He smiled again, a gruesome expression, then vanished.

Feeling wrung out, Kelsier slumped alongside the pool, lying on the stones—which actually felt a little like real stone, instead of the fluffy softness of everything else made of mist.

He hated this feeling of ignorance. Everyone else was in on some grand joke, and he was the butt.

Kelsier stared up at the ceiling, bathed in the glow of the shimmering Well and its column of light. Eventually, he came to a quiet decision.

He would find the answers.

In the Pits of Hathsin, he had awakened to purpose and had determined to destroy the Lord Ruler. Well, he would awaken again. He stood up and stepped into the light, strengthened. The clash of these gods was important, that thing in the Well dangerous. There was more to all of this than he'd ever known, and because of that he had a reason to live.

Perhaps more importantly, he had a reason to stay sane.

2

Kelsier no longer worried about madness or bore-dom. Each time he grew weary of his imprisonment, he remembered that feeling—that *humiliation*—he'd felt at Drifter's hands. Yes, he was trapped in a space only five or so feet across, but there was *plenty* to do.

First he returned to his study of the thing Beyond. He forced himself to duck beneath the light to face it and meet its inscrutable gaze—he did it until he didn't flinch when it turned its attention on him.

Ruin. A fitting name for that vast sense of erosion, decay, and destruction.

He continued to follow the Well's pulses. These trips gave him cryptic clues to Ruin's motives and plots. He sensed a familiar pattern to the things it changed—for Ruin seemed to be doing what Kelsier himself had done: co-opting a religion. Ruin was manipulating the hearts of the people by changing their lore and books.

That terrified Kelsier. His purpose expanded, as he

watched the world through these pulses. He didn't just need to understand, he needed to fight this thing. This horrible force that would end all things, if it could.

He struggled, therefore, with a desperation to understand what he saw. Why did Ruin transform the old Terris prophecies? What was the Drifter—whom Kelsier spotted in very rare pulses—doing up in the Terris Dominance? Who was this mysterious Mistborn to whom Ruin paid so much attention, and was he a threat to Vin?

When he rode the pulses, Kelsier watched for—*craved*—signs of the people he knew and loved. Ruin was keenly interested in Vin, and many of his pulses centered around watching her or the man she loved, that Elend Venture.

The mounting clues worried Kelsier. Armies around Luthadel. A city still in chaos. And—he hated to confront this one—it looked like the Venture boy was *king*. When Kelsier realized this, he was so angry he spent days away from the pulses.

They'd gone and put a *nobleman* in charge.

Yes, Kelsier had saved this man's life. Against his better judgment, he'd rescued the man that Vin loved. Out of love for her, perhaps a twisted paternal sense of duty. The Venture boy hadn't been *too* bad, compared to the rest of his kind. But to give him the throne? It seemed that even Dox was listening to Venture. Kelsier would have expected Breeze to ride whatever wind came his way, but Dockson?

Kelsier fumed, but he could not remain away for long. He hungered for these glimpses of his friends. Though each was only a brief flash—like a single image from eyes blinked open—he clung to them. They were reminders that outside his prison, life continued.

Occasionally he was given a glimpse of someone else. His brother, Marsh.

Marsh *lived*. That was a welcome discovery. Unfortunately, the discovery was tainted. For Marsh was an Inquisitor.

The two of them had never been what one would call familial. They had taken divergent paths in life, but that wasn't the true source of the distance between them—it wasn't even due to Marsh's stern ways butting against Kelsier's glibness, or Marsh's unspoken jealousy for things Kelsier had.

No, the truth was they had been raised knowing that at any point they could be dragged before the Inquisitors and murdered for their half-blooded nature. Each had reacted differently to an entire life spent, essentially, with a death sentence: Marsh with quiet tension and caution, Kelsier with aggressive self-confidence to mask his secrets.

Both had known a single, inescapable truth. If one brother were caught, it meant the other would be exposed as a half-blood and likely killed as well. Perhaps this situation would have brought other siblings together. Kelsier was ashamed to admit that for him and Marsh, it had been a wedge. Each mention of

"Stay safe" or "Watch yourself" had been colored by an undercurrent of "Don't screw up, or you'll get me killed." It had been a vast relief when, after their parents' deaths, the two of them had agreed to give up pretense and enter the underground of Luthadel.

At times Kelsier toyed with fantasies of what might have been. Could he and Marsh have integrated fully, becoming part of noble society? Could he have overcome his loathing for them and their culture?

Regardless, he wasn't fond of Marsh. The word "fond" sounded too much of walks in a park or time spent eating pastries. One was fond of a favorite book. No, Kelsier was not *fond* of Marsh. But strangely, he still loved him. He was initially happy to find the man alive, but then perhaps death would have been better than what had been done to him.

It took Kelsier weeks to figure out the reason Ruin was so interested in Marsh. Ruin could *talk* to Marsh. Marsh and other Inquisitors, judging by the glimpses and the sensation he received of words being sent.

How? Why Inquisitors? Kelsier found no answers in the visions he saw, though he did witness an important event.

The thing called Ruin was growing stronger, and it was stalking Vin and Elend. Kelsier saw it clearly in a trip through the pulses. A vision of the boy, Elend Venture, sleeping in his tent. The power of Ruin coalescing, forming a figure, malevolent and dangerous. It waited there until Vin entered, then tried to stab Elend.

As Kelsier lost the pulse, he was left with the image of Vin deflecting the blow and saving Elend. But he was confused. Ruin had waited there specifically until Vin returned.

It hadn't actually wanted to hurt Elend. It had just wanted Vin to see him trying.

Why?

3

It's a plug," Kelsier said.

Fuzz—Preservation, as the god had said he could be called—sat outside the prison. He was still missing half his face, and the rest of him was leaking in larger patches as well.

These days the god spent more time near the Well, for which Kelsier was grateful. He had been practicing how to pull information from the creature.

"Hmmm?" Preservation asked.

"This Well," Kelsier said, gesturing around him. "It's like a plug. You created a prison for Ruin, but even the most solid of burrows must have an entrance. *This* is that entrance, sealed with your own power to keep him out, since you two are opposites."

"That . . ." Preservation said, trailing off.

"That?" Kelsier prompted.

"That's *utterly wrong.*"

Damn, Kelsier thought. He'd spent weeks on that theory.

He was starting to feel an urgency. The pulses of the Well were growing more demanding, and Ruin seemed to be growing increasingly eager in its touch upon the world. Recently the light of the Well had started to act differently, condensing somehow, pulling together. Something was happening.

"We are gods, Kelsier," Preservation said with a voice that trailed off, then grew louder, then trailed off again. "We permeate everything. The rocks are me. The people are me. And him. All things persist, but decay. Ruin . . . and Preservation . . ."

"You told me this was your power," Kelsier said, gesturing again at the Well, trying to get the god back on topic. "That it gathers here."

"Yes, and elsewhere," Preservation said. "But yes, here. Like dew collects, my power gathers in that spot. It is natural. A cycle: clouds, rain, river, humidity. You cannot press so much essence into a system without it congealing here and there."

Great. That didn't tell him anything. He pressed further on the topic, but Fuzz grew quiet, so he tried something else. He needed to keep Preservation talking—to prevent the god from slumping into one of his quiet stupors.

"Are you afraid?" Kelsier asked. "If Ruin gets free, are you afraid he will kill you?"

"Ha," Preservation said. "I've told you. He killed me long, long ago."

"I find that hard to believe."

"Why?"

"Because I'm sitting here talking to you."

"And I'm talking to *you*. How alive are you?"

A good point.

"Death for one such as me is not like death for one such as you," Preservation said, staring off again. "I was killed long ago, when I made the decision to break our promise. But this power I hold . . . it *persists* and it *remembers*. It wants to be alive itself. I have died, but some of me remains. Enough to know that . . . there *were* plans. . . ."

It was no use trying to pry out what those plans were. He didn't remember whatever this "plan" was that he'd made.

"So it's not a plug," Kelsier said. "Then what is it?"

Preservation didn't reply. He didn't even seem to hear.

"You said to me once before," Kelsier continued, speaking more loudly, "that the power exists to be used. That it *needs* to be used. Why?"

Again no answer. He was going to need to try a different tactic. "I looked at him again. Your opposite."

Preservation stood up straight, turning his haunting, half-finished gaze upon Kelsier. Mentioning Ruin often shocked him out of his stupor.

"He is dangerous," Preservation said. "Stay away. My power protects you. Do not taunt him."

"Why? He's locked up."

"Nothing is eternal, not even time itself," Preservation said. "I didn't imprison him so much as *delay* him."

"And the power?"

"Yes . . ." Preservation said, nodding.

"Yes, what?"

"Yes, he will use that. I see." Preservation started, as if realizing—or maybe just recalling—something important. "My power created his prison. My power can unlock it. But how would he find someone who would do it? Who would hold the powers of creation, then *give them away* . . ."

"Which . . . we don't want them to do," Kelsier said.

"No. It will free him!"

"And last time?" Kelsier asked.

"Last time . . ." Preservation blinked, and seemed to come to himself more. "Yes, last time. The Lord Ruler. I made it work last time. I've put her into the spot to do this, but I can hear her thoughts. . . . He's been working on her. . . . So mixed up . . ."

"Fuzz?" Kelsier asked, uncertain.

"I must stop her. Someone . . ." His eyes unfocused.

"What are you doing?"

"Hush," Fuzz said, voice suddenly more commanding. "I'm trying to stop this."

Kelsier looked around, but there was nobody else here. "Who?"

"Do not assume that the me you see here is the only me," Fuzz said. "I am everywhere."

"But—"

"Hush!"

Kelsier hushed, in part because he was happy to see such strength from the god after so long motionless. After some time, however, he slumped down. "No use," Fuzz mumbled. "His tools are stronger."

"So . . ." Kelsier said, testing to see if he'd be hushed again. "Last time. Rashek used the power, instead of . . . what? Giving it up?"

Fuzz nodded. "Alendi would have done the right thing, as he perceived it. Given the power up—but that would have freed Ruin. 'Giving the power up' is a stand-in for giving the power to him. The powers would interpret that as me releasing him. My power, accepting his touch back into the world, directly."

"Great," Kelsier said. "We need a sacrifice then. Someone to take up the powers of eternity, then use them for whatever he wants instead of giving them away. Well, that is a sacrifice *I'm* perfect to make. How do I do it?"

Preservation regarded him. The creature's earlier strength was no more. He was fading, losing his human attributes. He didn't blink anymore, for example, and didn't make a pretense of breathing in before speaking. He could be utterly motionless, lifeless as an iron rod.

"You," Preservation finally said. "Using *my* power. *You.*"

"You let the Lord Ruler do it."

"He tried to save the world."

"As did I."

"You tried to rescue a boatful of people from a fire by sinking the boat, then claiming, 'At least they didn't burn to death.'" God hesitated. "You're going to punch me again, aren't you?"

"Can't reach you, Fuzz," Kelsier said. "The power. *How do I use it?*"

"You can't," Preservation said. "That power is part of the prison. This is what you did by merging your soul to the Well, Kelsier. You wouldn't be able to hold it anyway. You're not Connected enough to me."

Kelsier settled down to think on this, but before he had time to do much, he noticed an oddity. Were those *figures* in the chamber outside? Yes, they were. Living people, marked by their glowing souls. More Inquisitors come to drop off a dead body? He hadn't seen any of them for ages.

Two people stole into the corridor and approached the Well, passing rows of pillars that showed as illusory mist to Kelsier.

"They're here," Preservation said.

"Who?" Kelsier said, squinting. It was difficult to make out details of faces, with those souls glowing. "Is that . . ."

It was Vin.

"What?" Preservation said, looking toward Kelsier,

noting his shock. "You thought I was waiting here for nothing? It happens today. The Well of Ascension is full. The time has arrived."

The other figure was the boy, Elend Venture. Kelsier was surprised to find he wasn't angry at the sight. Yes, the crew should have known better than to put a nobleman in charge, but that wasn't really Elend's fault. He'd always been too oblivious to be dangerous.

Besides, whatever the faults of his parentage, this Venture boy had stayed with Vin.

Kelsier folded his arms, watching Venture kneel beside the pool. "If he touches it, I'm going to slap him."

"He will not," Preservation said. "It's for her. He knows it. I've been preparing her. I tried, at least."

Vin turned, and seemed to be looking at God. Yes, she *could* see him. Was there a way Kelsier could use that?

"You tried?" Kelsier said. "Did you explain what she needs to do? Your opposite has been watching her, interacting with her. I've *seen* him doing it. He tried to kill Elend."

"No," Fuzz said, haunted. "He was imitating me. He looked as I do, to them, and tried to kill the boy. Not because he cares about one death, but because he wanted her to distrust me. To think I am her enemy. But can't she tell the difference? Between his hate and destruction, and my peace. I cannot kill. I've never been able to kill. . . ."

"Talk to her!" Kelsier said. "Tell her what she needs to do, Fuzz!"

"I . . ." Preservation shook his head. "I can't get through to her, can't speak to her. I can hear her mind, Kelsier. His lies are there. She doesn't trust me. She thinks she needs to give it up. I've tried to stop this. I left her clues, and then I tried to make someone else stop her. But . . . I've . . . I've failed . . ."

Oh, hell, Kelsier thought. *Need a plan. Quick.*

Vin was going to give up the power. Release the thing. Even without Preservation's assertions, Kelsier would have known what Vin would do. She was a better person than he had ever been, and she never *had* thought she deserved the rewards she was given. She'd take this power, and she'd assume she had to give it up for the greater good.

But how to change that? If Preservation couldn't speak to her, then what?

Elend stood up and approached Preservation. Yes, the boy could see Preservation too.

"She needs motivation," Kelsier said, an idea clicking in his mind. Ruin had tried to stab Elend, to frighten her.

It was the right idea. He just hadn't gone far enough.

"Stab him," Kelsier said.

"What?" Preservation said, aghast.

Kelsier pushed out of his prison bonds a few steps, approaching Fuzz, who stood just outside. He strained to the absolute limits of his fetters.

"Stab him," Kelsier said. "Use that knife at your belt, Fuzz. They can see you, and you can affect their world. *Stab Elend Venture.* Give her a reason to use the power. She'll want to save him."

"I'm *Preservation,*" he said. "The knife . . . I haven't actually drawn it in millennia. You speak of acting like him, as he pretended I would act! It's horrible!"

"You have to!" Kelsier said.

"I can't . . . I . . ." Fuzz reached to his belt, and his hand shimmered. The knife appeared there. He looked down at it, the blade glistening. "Old friend . . ." he whispered at it.

He looked toward Elend, who nodded. Preservation raised his arm, weapon in hand.

Then stopped.

His half face was a mask of pain. "No . . ." he whispered. "I Preserve . . ."

He's not going to do it, Kelsier thought, watching Elend talk to Vin, his posture reassuring. *He can't do it.*

Only one option.

"Sorry, kid," Kelsier said.

Kelsier grabbed Preservation's shimmering arm and *slashed* it across the Venture boy's stomach.

He felt as if he were stabbing his own flesh. Not because of Venture, but because he knew what it would do to Vin. His heart lurched as she rushed to Venture's side, weeping.

Well, he'd saved this boy's life once, so this would make them even. Besides, she would rescue him. She'd *have* to save Elend. She loved him.

Kelsier stepped back, returning to his prison proper,

leaving an aghast Preservation to stare at his own hand as he stumbled away from the fallen man.

"Gut wound," Kelsier whispered. "He'll take time to die, Vin. Grab the power. It's *right here*. Use it."

She cradled Venture. Kelsier waited, anxious. If she entered the pool, she'd be able to see Kelsier, wouldn't she? She'd become transcendent, like Preservation. Or would she have to use the power first?

Would that free Kelsier? He had no answers, only an assurance that whatever happened, he could not let that thing Beyond escape. He turned.

And was shocked to find it *there*. He could sense it, pressed against the reality of this world, an infinite darkness. Not just the flimsy imitation of Preservation he'd made before, but the entire vast power. It wasn't in any specific space, but at the same time it was pressed up against reality and watching with a keen interest.

To his horror, Kelsier saw it change, sending forward spines like the spindly legs of a spider. On their end, dangling like a puppet, was a humanoid figure.

Vin . . . it whispered. *Vin . . .*

She looked toward the pool, her posture grieved. Then she left Venture and entered the Well, passing Kelsier without seeing him and reaching the deepest point. She sank slowly into the light. At the last moment, she ripped something glowing from her ear and tossed it out—a bit of metal. Her earring?

Once she sank completely, she did not appear on

this side. Instead, a storm began. A rising column of light surrounded Kelsier, blocking him from seeing anything but the raw *energy*. Like a sudden tide, an explosion, an instant sunrise. It was all around him, active, *excited*.

You mustn't do it, child, Ruin said through his human-like puppet. How could it speak with such a soothing voice? He could see the force behind it, the destruction, but the face it put on was so kindly. *You know what you must do.*

"Don't listen to it, Vin!" Kelsier screamed, but his voice was lost in the roar of the power. He shouted and railed as the voice conned Vin, warning her that if she took the power she'd destroy the world. Kelsier fought through the light, trying to find her, to seize her and explain.

He failed. He failed *horribly*. He couldn't make himself heard, couldn't touch Vin. Couldn't do anything. Even his impromptu plan of stabbing Elend proved foolish, for she released the power. Weeping, flayed, ripped open, she did the most selfless thing he had ever seen.

And in so doing, she doomed them.

The power became a weapon as she released it. It made a spear in the air and ripped a hole through reality and into the place where Ruin waited.

Ruin rushed through that hole to freedom.

4

Kelsier sat on the lip of the now empty Well of Ascension. The light was gone, and with it his prison. He could leave.

He didn't seem to be stretching away and fading. Apparently being part of Preservation's power for a time had expanded Kelsier's soul, letting him linger. Though honestly, he wished he could vanish at this moment.

Vin—glowing and radiant to his eyes—lay beside Elend Venture, clutching him and weeping as his soul pulsed, growing weaker. Kelsier stood up, turning his back toward the sight. For all his cleverness, he'd gone and broken the poor girl's heart.

I must be the smartest idiot around, Kelsier thought.

"It was going to happen," Preservation said. "I thought . . . Maybe . . ." From the corner of his eye, Kelsier saw Fuzz approach Vin, then look down at the fallen Venture.

"I can Preserve him," Preservation whispered.

Kelsier spun. Preservation started waving at Vin,

and she stumbled to her feet. She followed the god a few feet to something Elend had dropped, a fallen nugget of metal. Where had that come from?

The Venture boy was carrying it when he entered, Kelsier thought. That was the last bit of metal from the other side of the room, the twin of the one the Drifter had stolen. Kelsier approached as Vin took the nugget of metal, so tiny, and approached Elend, then put it into his mouth. She washed it down with a vial of metal.

Soul and metal became one. Elend's light strengthened, glowing vibrantly. Kelsier closed his eyes, feeling a thrumming sense of peace.

"That was good work, Fuzz," Kelsier said, opening his eyes and smiling at Preservation as the god stepped over to him. Vin's posture manifested incredible joy. "I'm almost ready to think you're a benevolent god."

"Stabbing him was dangerous, painful," Preservation said. "I cannot condone such recklessness. But perhaps it was right, regardless of how I feel."

"Ruin's free," Kelsier said, looking upward. "That thing has escaped."

"Yes. Fortunately, before I died, I put a plan into motion. I can't remember it, but I'm certain that it was brilliant."

"You know, I've said something similar myself on occasion, after a night of drinking." Kelsier rubbed his chin. "I'm free too."

"Yes."

"This is where you joke that you aren't certain which was more dangerous to release. Me or the other one."

"No," Fuzz said. "I know which is more dangerous."

"Failing marks for effort there, I'm afraid."

"But perhaps . . ." Preservation said. "Perhaps I cannot say which is more *annoying*." He smiled. With his face half melted off and his neck starting to go, it was unnerving. Like a happy bark from a crippled puppy.

Kelsier slapped him on the shoulder. "We'll make a solid crewmember out of you yet, Fuzz. For now, I want to get the *hell* out of this room."

PART THREE
SPIRIT

1

Kelsier really wanted something to drink. Wasn't that what you did when you got out of prison? Went drinking, enjoyed your freedom by giving it up to a little booze and a terrible headache?

When alive, he'd usually avoided such levity. He liked to control a situation, not let it control him— but he couldn't deny that he thirsted for something to drink, to numb the experience he'd just been through.

That seemed terribly unfair. No body, but he could still be thirsty?

He climbed from the caverns surrounding the Well of Ascension, passing through misty chambers and tunnels. As before, when he touched something he was able to see what it looked like in the real world.

His footing was firm on the inconstant ground; though it was somewhat springy, like cloth, it held his weight unless he stamped hard—which would cause his foot to sink in like it was pushing through thick mud. He could even pass through the walls if he tried, but it was harder than it had been during his initial run, when he'd been dying.

He emerged from the caverns into the basement of Kredik Shaw, the Lord Ruler's palace. It was even easier than usual to get turned about in this place, as everything was misty to his eyes. He touched the things of mist that he passed, so he could picture his surroundings better. A vase, a carpet, a door.

Kelsier eventually stepped out onto the streets of Luthadel a free—if dead—man. For a time he just walked the city, so relieved to be out of that hole that he was able to ignore the sense of dread he felt at Ruin's escape.

He must have wandered an entire day that way, sitting on rooftops, strolling past fountains. Looking over this city dotted with glowing pieces of metal, like lights hovering in the mists at night. He ended up on top of the city wall, observing the koloss who had set up camp outside the town but—somehow—didn't seem to be killing anyone.

He needed to see if there was a way to contact his friends. Unfortunately, without the pulses—those had stopped when Ruin escaped—to guide him, he didn't know where to start looking. He'd lost track of Vin and Elend in his excitement at leaving the caverns, but he remembered some of what he'd seen through the pulses. That gave him a few places to search.

He ultimately found his crew at Keep Venture. It was the day after the disaster at the Well of Ascension, and they appeared to be holding a funeral. Kelsier strolled through the courtyard, passing among the glowing souls of men, each burning like a limelight. Those he brushed gave him an impression of their appearance. Many he recognized: skaa he'd interacted with, encouraged, uplifted during his final months of life. Others were unfamiliar. A disturbing number of soldiers who had once served the Lord Ruler.

He found Vin at the front, sitting on the steps of Keep Venture, huddled and slumped over. Elend was nowhere to be seen, though Ham stood nearby, arms folded. In the courtyard, somebody waved their hands before the group, giving a speech. Was that Demoux? Leading the people in the funeral service? Those were certainly corpses laid out in the courtyard, their souls no longer shining. He couldn't hear what Demoux was saying, but the presentation seemed clear.

Kelsier settled down on the steps beside Vin. He clasped his hands before himself. "So . . . that went well."

Vin, of course, didn't reply.

"I mean," Kelsier continued, "yes, we ended up releasing a worldending force of destruction and chaos, but at least the Lord Ruler is dead. Mission accomplished. Plus you still have your nobleman boyfriend, so there's that. Don't worry about the scar on his stomach. It'll make him look more rugged. Mists know, the little bookworker could use some toughening up."

She didn't move, but maintained her slumped posture. He rested his arm across her shoulders and was given a glimpse of her as she looked in the real world. Full of color and life, yet somehow ... weathered. She seemed so much older now, no longer the child he'd found scamming obligators on the streets.

He leaned down beside her. "I'm going to beat this thing, Vin. I *am* going take care of this."

"And how," Preservation said from the courtyard below the steps, "are you going to accomplish *that*?"

Kelsier looked up. Though he was prepared for the sight of Preservation, he still winced to see him as he was—barely even in human shape any longer, more a dissolved bunch of weaving threads of frayed smoke, giving the vague impression of a head, arms, legs.

"He's free," Preservation said. "That's it. Time up. Contract due. He will take what was promised."

"We'll stop him."

"Stop him? He's the force of entropy, a universal constant. You can't *stop* that any more than you can stop time."

Kelsier stood up, leaving Vin and walking down the steps toward Preservation. He wished he could hear what Demoux was saying to this small crowd of glowing souls.

"If he can't be stopped," Kelsier said, "then we'll slow him. You did it before, right? Your grand plan?"

"I . . ." Preservation said. "Yes . . . There was a plan. . . ."

"I'm free now. I can help you put it into motion."

"Free?" Preservation laughed. "No, you've just entered a larger prison. Tied to this Realm, bound to it. There's nothing you can do. Nothing I can do."

"That—"

"He's watching us, you know," Preservation said, looking upward at the sky.

Kelsier followed his gaze reluctantly. The sky—misty and shifting—seemed so distant. It felt as if it had pulled back from the planet, like people in a crowd shying away from a corpse. In that vastness Kelsier saw something dark, thrashing, writhing upon itself. More solid than mist, like an ocean of snakes, obscuring the tiny sun.

He knew that vastness. Ruin was indeed watching.

"He thinks you're insignificant," Preservation said. "I think he finds you amusing—the soul of Ati that is still in there somewhere would laugh at this."

"He has a soul?"

Preservation didn't respond. Kelsier stepped up to him, passing corpses made of mists on the ground.

"If he is alive," Kelsier said, "then he can be killed. No matter how powerful." *You're proof of that, Fuzz. He's killing you.*

Preservation laughed, a harsh, barking noise. "You keep forgetting which of us is a god and which is just a poor dead shadow. Waiting to expire." He waved a mostly unraveled arm, fingers made of spirals of unwound, misty strings. "Listen to them. Doesn't it embarrass you how they talk? The Survivor? Ha! I

Preserved them for millennia. What have *you* done for them?"

Kelsier turned toward Demoux. Preservation appeared to have forgotten that Kelsier couldn't hear the speech. Intending to go touch Demoux, to get a view of what he looked like now, Kelsier brushed one of the corpses on the ground.

A young man. A soldier, by the looks of it. He didn't know the boy, but he started to worry. He looked back at where Ham was standing—that figure near him would be Breeze.

What of the others?

He grew cold, then started touching corpses, looking for any he recognized. His motions became more frantic.

"What are you seeking?" Preservation asked.

"How many—" Kelsier swallowed. "How many of these were friends of mine?"

"Some," Preservation said.

"Any members of the crew?"

"No," Preservation said, and Kelsier let out a sigh. "No, they died during the initial break-in, days ago. Dockson. Clubs."

A spear of ice shot through Kelsier. He tried to stand up from beside the corpse he'd been inspecting, but stumbled, trying to force out the words. "No. No, not Dox."

Preservation nodded.

"Wh . . . When did it happen? How?"

Preservation laughed. The sound of madness. He showed little of the kindly, uncertain man who had greeted Kelsier when he'd first entered this place.

"Both were murdered by koloss as the siege broke. Their bodies were burned days ago, Kelsier, while you were trapped."

Kelsier trembled, feeling lost. "I . . ." Kelsier said.

Dox. I wasn't here for him. I could have seen him again, as he passed. Talked to him. Saved him maybe?

"He cursed you as he died, Kelsier," Preservation said, voice harsh. "He blamed you for all this."

Kelsier bowed his head. Another lost friend. And Clubs too . . . two good men. He'd lost too many of those in his life, dammit. Far too many.

I'm sorry, Dox, Clubs. I'm sorry for failing you.

Kelsier took that anger, that bitterness and shame, and channeled it. He'd found purpose again during his days in prison. He wouldn't lose it now.

He stood and turned to Preservation. The god— shockingly—cringed as if *frightened*. Kelsier seized the god's form, and in a brief moment was given a vision of the grandness beyond. The pervading light of Preservation that permeated all things. The world, the mists, the metals, the very souls of men. This creature was somehow dying, but his power was far from gone.

He also felt Preservation's pain. It was the loss Kelsier had felt at Dox's death, only magnified thousands of times over. Preservation felt every light that went out, felt them and knew them as a person he had loved.

Around the world they were dying at an accelerated pace. Too much ash was falling, and Preservation only anticipated it increasing. Armies of koloss rampaging beyond control. Death, destruction, a world on its last legs.

And . . . to the south . . . what was *that*? People?

Kelsier held Preservation, in awe at this creature's divine agony. Then Kelsier pulled him close, into an embrace.

"I'm so sorry," Kelsier whispered.

"Oh, Senna . . ." Preservation whispered. "I'm losing this place. Losing them all . . ."

"We are going to stop it," Kelsier said, pulling back.

"It can't be stopped. The deal . . ."

"Deals can be broken."

"Not these kinds of deals, Kelsier. I was able to trick Ruin before, lock him away, by fooling him with our agreement. But that wasn't a breach of contract, more leaving a hole in the agreement to be exploited. This time there are no holes."

"Then we go out kicking and screaming," Kelsier said. "You and me, we're a team."

Preservation seemed to *condense*, his form pulling itself together, threads reweaving. "A team. Yes. A crew."

"To do the impossible."

"Defy reality," Preservation whispered. "Everyone always said you were insane."

"And I always acknowledged that they had a point," Kelsier said. "Thing is, while they were correct to question my sanity, they never did have the right reasoning. It's not my ambition that should worry them."

"Then what should?"

Kelsier smiled.

Preservation, in turn, laughed—a sound that had lost its edge, the harshness gone. "I can't help you do . . . whatever it is you think you're doing. Not directly. I don't . . . think well enough anymore. But . . ."

"But?"

Preservation solidified a little further. "But I know where you'll find someone who can."

2

Kelsier followed a thread of Preservation, like a glowing tendril of mist, through the city. He made sure to look up periodically, confronting that force in the sky, which had boiled through the mists there and was coming to dominate in every direction.

Kelsier would not back down. He would not let this thing intimidate him again. He'd already killed one god. The second murder was always easier than the first.

The tendril of Preservation led him past shadowy tenements, through a slum that somehow looked even more depressing on this side—all crammed together, the souls of men packed in frightened lumps. His crew had saved this city, but many of the people Kelsier passed didn't seem to know it yet.

Eventually the tendril led him out broken city gates to the north, past rubble and corpses being slowly sorted. Past living armies and that fearsome army of koloss, out beyond the city and a short hike along the river to . . . the lake?

Luthadel was built not far from the lake that bore its name, though most of the city's populace determinedly ignored that fact. Lake Luthadel wasn't the swimming or sport kind of lake, unless you fancied bathing in a soupy sludge that was more ash than it was water—and good luck catching what few fish remained after centuries of residing next to a city full of half-starved skaa. This close to the ashmounts, keeping the river and lake navigable had demanded the full-time attention of an entire class of people, the canal workers, a strange breed of skaa who rarely mixed with those from the city proper.

They would have been horrified to find that here on this side, the lake—and actually the river as well— was inverted somehow. Opposite to the way the mists under his feet had a liquid feel to them, the lake rose into a solid mound, only a few inches high but harder and somehow more substantial than the ground he'd become used to walking upon.

In fact, the lake was like a low island rising from the sea of mists. What was solid and what was fluid seemed somehow reversed in this place. Kelsier stepped up to the island's edge, the ribbon of Preservation's essence curling past him and leading onto the island, like a mythical string showing the way home from the grand maze of Ishathon.

Kelsier stuffed his hands in his trouser pockets and kicked at the ground of the island. It was some type of dark, smoky stone.

"What?" Preservation whispered.

Kelsier jumped, then glanced at the line of light. "You . . . in there, Fuzz?"

"I'm everywhere," Preservation said, his voice soft, frail. He sounded exhausted. "Why have you stopped?"

"This is different."

"Yes, it congeals here," Preservation said. "It has to do with the way men think, and where they are likely to pass. Somewhat to do with that, at least."

"But what is it?" Kelsier said, stepping up onto the island.

Preservation said nothing further, and so Kelsier continued toward the center of the island. Whatever had "congealed" here, it was strikingly stonelike. And things grew on it. Kelsier passed scrubby plants sprouting from the otherwise hard ground—not misty, inchoate plants, but real ones full of color. They had broad brown leaves with—curiously—what seemed like *mist* rising from them. None of the plants reached higher than his knees, but there were still far more than he'd expected to find here.

As he passed through a field of the plants, he thought he caught something scurrying between them, rustling leaves in its passing.

The world of the dead has plants and animals? he

thought. But that wasn't what Preservation had called it. The Cognitive Realm. How did these plants grow here? What watered them?

The farther he penetrated onto this island, the darker it became. Ruin was covering up that tiny sun, and Kelsier began to miss even the faint glow that had permeated the phantom mists in the city. Soon he was traveling in what seemed like twilight.

Eventually Preservation's ribbon grew thin, then vanished. Kelsier stopped near its tip, whispering, "Fuzz? You there?"

No response, the silence refuting Preservation's claim earlier that he was everywhere. Kelsier shook his head. Perhaps Preservation was listening, but wasn't *there* enough to give a reply. Kelsier continued forward, passing through a place where the plants had grown to waist height, mist rising from their broad leaves like steam from a hot plate.

Finally, ahead he spotted *light*. Kelsier pulled up. He'd fallen into a prowl naturally, led by instincts gained from a life spent on the con, literally since the day of his birth. He had no weapons. He knelt, feeling at the ground for a stone or stick, but these plants weren't big enough to provide anything substantial, and the ground was smooth, unbroken.

Preservation had promised him help, but he wasn't sure how much he trusted what Preservation said. Odd, that living through his own death should make him *more* hesitant to trust in God's word. He took off his belt for a weapon, but it evaporated in his hands and appeared back on his waist. Shaking his head, he prowled closer, approaching near enough to the fire to pick out two people. Alive, and in this Realm, not glowing souls or misty spirits.

The man wore skaa clothing—suspenders, shirt with sleeves rolled up—and tended a small dinner fire. He had short hair and a narrow, almost pinched face. That knife at his belt, nearly long enough to be a sword, would come in very handy.

The other person, who sat on a small folding chair, might have been Terris. There were some among their population who had a skin tone almost as dark as hers, though he'd also met some people from the various southern dominances who were dark. She certainly wasn't wearing Terris clothing—she had on a sturdy brown dress, with a large leather girdle around the waist, and wore her hair woven into tiny braids.

Two. He could handle two, couldn't he? Even without Allomancy or weapons. Regardless, best to be careful. He hadn't forgotten his humiliation at the hands of the Drifter. Kelsier made a careful decision, then stood up, straightened his coat, and strode into their camp.

"Well," he proclaimed, "this has been an unusual few days, I can tell you *that*."

The man at the fire scrambled backward, hand on his knife, gaping. The woman remained seated, though she reached for something at her side. A little tube with a handle on the bottom. She pointed it toward him, treating it like some kind of weapon.

"So," Kelsier said, glancing at the sky with its shifting, writhing mass of too-solid tendrils, "anyone else bothered by the voracious force of destruction in the air above us?"

"Shadows!" the man shouted. "It's *you*. You're dead!"

"Depends on your definition of dead," Kelsier said, strolling over to the fire. The woman trailed him with that odd weapon of hers. "What in the blazes are you *burning* for that fire?" He looked up at the two of them. "What?"

"How?" the man sputtered. "What? When . . ."

". . . Why?" Kelsier added helpfully.

"Yes, why!"

"I have a very delicate constitution, you see," Kelsier said. "And death seemed like it would be *rather* bad for the digestion. So I decided not to participate."

"One doesn't merely *decide* to become a shadow!" the man exclaimed. He had a faintly strange accent, one Kelsier couldn't place. "It's an important rite! With requirements and traditions. This . . . this is . . ." He threw his hands into the air. "This is a *bother*."

Kelsier smiled, meeting the gaze of the woman, who reached for a cup of something warm on the ground beside her. With her other hand she tucked her weapon away, as if it had never been there. She was perhaps in her mid-thirties.

"The Survivor of Hathsin," she said, musing.

"You seem to have me at a disadvantage," Kelsier said. "One problem with notoriety, unfortunately."

"I should assume there are many disadvantages to fame, for a thief. One doesn't particularly wish to be recognized while trying to lift pocketbooks."

"Considering how he's regarded by the people of this domain," the man said, still watching Kelsier with a wary eye, "I'd expect them to be delighted to discover him robbing them."

"Yes," Kelsier said dryly, "they practically lined up for the privilege. Must I repeat myself?"

She considered. "My name is Khriss, of Taldain." She nodded toward the other man, and he reluctantly replaced his knife. "That is Nazh, a man in my employ."

"Excellent," Kelsier said. "Any idea why Preservation would tell me to come talk to you?"

"*Preservation?*" Nazh said, stepping up and seizing Kelsier's arm. So, as with the Drifter, they could indeed touch Kelsier. "You've spoken directly with one of the *Shards*?"

"Sure," Kelsier said. "Fuzz and I go way back." He pulled his arm free of Nazh's grip and grabbed the other folding stool from beside the fire—two simple pieces of wood that folded together, a piece of cloth between them to sit on.

He settled it across from Khriss and sat down.

"I don't like this, Khriss," Nazh said. "He's dangerous."

"Fortunately," she replied, "so are we. The Shard Preservation, Survivor. How does he look?"

"Is that a test to see if I've actually spoken with him," Kelsier said, "or a sincere question as to the creature's status?"

"Both."

"He's dying," Kelsier said, spinning Nazh's knife in his fingers. He'd palmed it during their altercation a moment ago, and was curious to find that though it was made of metal, it didn't glow. "He's a short man with black hair—or he used to be. He's been . . . well, *unraveling.*"

"Hey," Nazh said, eyes narrowing at the knife. He looked at his belt, and the empty sheath. "*Hey!*"

"Unraveling," Khriss said. "So a slow death. Ati doesn't know how to Splinter another Shard? Or he hasn't the strength? Hmm . . ."

"Ati?" Kelsier asked. "Preservation mentioned that name too."

Khriss pointed at the sky with one finger while she sipped at her drink. "That's him. What he's become, at least."

"And . . . what is a Shard?" Kelsier asked.

"Are you a scholar, Mr. Survivor?"

"No," he said. "But I've killed a few."

"Cute. Well, you've stumbled into something far, far bigger than you, your politics, or your little planet."

"Bigger than you can handle, Survivor," Nazh said,

swiping back his knife as Kelsier balanced it on his finger. "You should just bow out now."

"Nazh does have a point," Khriss said. "Your questions are dangerous. Once you step behind the curtain and see the actors as the people they are, it becomes harder to pretend the play is real."

"I . . ." Kelsier leaned forward, clasping his hands before him. Hell . . . that fire was warm, but it didn't seem to be *burning* anything. He stared at the flames and swallowed. "I woke up from death after having, deep down, expected there to be no afterlife. I found that God was real, but that he was dying. I need answers. *Please.*"

"Curious," she said.

He looked up, frowning.

"I have heard many stories of you, Survivor," she said. "They often laud your many admirable qualities. Sincerity is never one of those."

"I can steal something else from your manservant," Kelsier said, "if it will make you feel more comfortable that I am what you expected."

"You can try," Nazh said, walking around the fire, folding his arms and obviously trying to look intimidating.

"The Shards," Khriss said, drawing Kelsier's attention, "are not God, but they are *pieces* of God. Ruin, Preservation, Autonomy, Cultivation, Devotion . . . There are sixteen of them."

"Sixteen," Kelsier breathed. "There are fourteen *more* of these things running around?"

"The rest are on other planets."

"Other . . ." Kelsier blinked. "Other *planets.*"

"Ah, see," Nazh said. "You've broken him already, Khriss."

"Other planets," she repeated gently. "Yes, there are dozens of them. Many are inhabited by people much like you or me. There is an original, shrouded and hidden somewhere in the cosmere. I've yet to find it, but I *have* found stories.

"Anyway, there was a God. Adonalsium. I don't know if it was a force or a being, though I suspect the latter. Sixteen people, together, *killed* Adonalsium, ripping it apart and dividing its essence between them, becoming the first who Ascended."

"Who were they?" Kelsier said, trying to make sense of this.

"A diverse group," she said. "With equally diverse motives. Some wished for the power; others saw killing Adonalsium as the only good option left to them. Together they murdered a deity, and became divine themselves." She smiled in a kindly way, as if to prepare him for what came next. "Two of those created this planet, Survivor, including the people on it."

"So . . . my world, and everyone I know," Kelsier said, "is the creation of a pair of . . . half gods?"

"More like fractional gods," Nazh said. "And ones with no particular qualifications for deityhood, other than being conniving enough to murder the guy who had the job before."

"Oh, hell . . ." Kelsier breathed. "No wonder we're all so bloody messed up."

"Actually," Khriss noted, "people are generally like that, no matter who made them. If it's any consolation, Adonalsium originally created the first humans, therefore your gods had a pattern to use."

"So we're copies of a flawed original," Kelsier said. "Not terribly comforting." He looked upward. "And that thing? It used to be human?"

"The power . . . distorts," Khriss said. "There's a person in that somewhere, directing it. Or perhaps just riding it at this point."

Kelsier remembered the puppet Ruin had presented, the shape of a man. Now basically a shell filled with a terrible power. "So what happens if one of these things . . . dies?"

"I'm very curious to see," Khriss said. "I've never viewed it in person, and the past deaths were different. They were each a single, stunning event, the god's power shattered and dispersed. This is more like a strangulation, while those were like a beheading. This should be very instructive."

"Unless I stop it," Kelsier said.

She smiled at him.

"Don't be patronizing," Kelsier snapped, standing

up, the stool falling down behind him. "I am going to stop it."

"This world is winding down, Survivor," Khriss said. "It is a true shame, but I know of no way to save it. I came with the hopes that I might be able to help, but I can't even reach the Physical Realm here any longer."

"Someone destroyed the gateway in," Nazh noted. "Someone *incredibly* foolhardy. Brash. Stupid. Didn't—"

"You're overselling it," Kelsier said. "The Drifter told me what I did."

"The . . . who?" Khriss asked.

"Fellow with white hair," Kelsier said. "Lanky, with a sharp nose and—"

"Damn," Khriss said. "Did he get to the Well of Ascension?"

"Stole something there," Kelsier said. "A bit of metal."

"*Damn,*" Khriss said, looking at her servant. "We need to go. I'm sorry, Survivor."

"But—"

"This isn't because of what you just told us," she said, rising and waving for Nazh to help gather their things. "We were leaving anyway. This planet is dying; as much as I wish to witness the death of a Shard, I don't dare risk doing it from up close. We'll observe from afar."

"Preservation thought you'd be able to help," Kelsier said. "Surely there is *something* you can do. Something you can tell me. It can't be over."

"I *am* sorry, Survivor," Khriss said softly. "Perhaps

if I knew more, perhaps if I could convince the Ey-ree to answer my questions . . ." She shook her head. "It will happen slowly, Survivor, over months. But it is coming. Ruin will consume this world, and the man once known as Ati won't be able to stop it. If he even cared to."

"Everything," Kelsier whispered. "Everything I've known. Every person on my . . . my planet?"

Nearby, Nazh bent down and picked up the fire, making it *vanish*. The oversized flame just folded up upon itself in his palm, and Kelsier thought he saw a puff of mist when it did so. Kelsier picked up his stool with one finger, unscrewed the bolt on the bottom, and palmed it into his hand before passing the stool to Nazh.

Nazh then tugged on a hiking pack, tied with scroll cases across the top. He looked to Khriss.

"Stay," Kelsier said, turning back to Khriss. "Help me."

"Help you? I can't even help *myself*, Survivor. I'm in exile, and even if I weren't I wouldn't have the re-sources to stop a Shard. I probably should never have come." She hesitated. "And I'm sorry, but I cannot in-vite you to come with us. The eyes of your god will be upon you, Kelsier. He'll know where you are, as you have pieces of him within. It has been dangerous enough to speak here with you."

Nazh handed her a pack, and she slung it over her shoulder.

"I *am* going to stop this," Kelsier told them.

Khriss lifted a hand and curled her fingers in an unfamiliar gesture, bidding him farewell it seemed. She turned away from the clearing and strode away, into the brush. Nazh followed.

Kelsier sank down. They'd taken the stools, so he settled onto the ground, bowing his head. *This is what you deserve, Kelsier,* a piece of him thought. *You wished to dance with the divine and steal from gods. Should you now be surprised that you've found yourself in over your head?*

The sound of rustling leaves made him scramble back to his feet. Nazh emerged from the shadows. The shorter man stopped at the perimeter of the abandoned camp, then cursed softly before stepping forward and removing his side knife, sheath and all, and handing it toward Kelsier.

Hesitant, Kelsier accepted the leatherbound weapon.

"It's a bad state you and yours are in," Nazh said softly, "but I rather like this place. Damnable mists and all." He pointed westward. "They've set up out there."

"They?"

"The Eyree," he said. "They've been at this far longer than we have, Survivor. If someone will know how to help you, it will be the Eyree. Look for them where the land becomes solid again."

"Solid again . . ." Kelsier said. "Lake Tyrian?"

"Beyond. Far beyond, Survivor."

"The *ocean*? That's miles and miles away. Past Farmost!"

Nazh patted him on the shoulder, then turned back to hike after Khriss.

"Is there hope?" Kelsier called.

"What if I told you no?" Nazh said over his shoulder. "What if I said I figured you were damn well ruined, so to speak. Would it change what you were going to do?"

"No."

Nazh raised his fingers to his forehead in a kind of salute. "Farewell, Survivor. Take care of my knife. I'm fond of it."

He vanished into the darkness. Kelsier watched after him, then did the only rational thing.

He ate the bolt he'd taken from the bottom of the stool.

3

The bolt didn't do anything. He'd hoped he'd be able to make Allomancy work, but the bolt just settled into his stomach—a strange and uncomfortable weight. He couldn't burn it, despite trying. As he walked, he eventually coughed it back up and tossed it away.

He stepped to the transition from the island to the misty ground around Luthadel, and felt a new weight upon him. A doomed world, dying gods, and an entire universe he'd never known existed. His only hope now was . . . to journey to the ocean?

That was farther than he had ever gone, even during his travels with Gemmel. It would take months to walk that far. Did they have months?

He stepped off the island, crossing onto the soft ground of the misted banks. Luthadel loomed in the near distance, a shadowy wall of curling mist.

"Fuzz?" he called. "You out there?"

"I'm everywhere," Preservation said, appearing beside him.

"So you were listening?" Kelsier asked.

He nodded absently, form frayed, face indistinct. "I think . . . Surely I was . . ."

"They mentioned someone called the Eyes Ree?"

"Yes, the I-ree," Preservation said, pronouncing it in a slightly different way. "Three letters. I R E. It means something in their language, these people from another land. The ones who died, but did not. I have felt them crowding at the edges of my vision, like spirits in the night."

"Dead, but alive," Kelsier said. "Like me?"

"No."

"Then what?"

"Died, but did not."

Great, Kelsier thought. He turned toward the west. "They are supposedly at the ocean."

"The Ire built a city," Preservation said softly. "In a place between worlds . . ."

"Well," Kelsier said, then took a deep breath. "That's where I'm going."

"Going?" Preservation said. "You're leaving me?"

The urgency of those words startled Kelsier. "If these people can help us, then I need to talk to them."

"They can't help us," Preservation said. "They're . . . they're callous. They plot over my corpse like scavenging insects waiting for the last beat of the heart. Don't go. Don't *leave me.*"

"You're everywhere. I can't leave you."

"No. They're beyond me. I . . . I cannot depart this land. I'm too Invested in it, in every rock and leaf." He pulsed, his already indistinct form spreading thinner. "We . . . grow attached easily, and it takes one who is particularly dedicated to leave."

"And Ruin?" Kelsier said, turning toward the west. "If he destroys everything, would he be able to escape?"

"Yes," Preservation said, very softly. "He could go then. But Kelsier, you can't abandon me. We . . . we're a team, right?"

Kelsier rested his hand on the creature's shoulder. Once so confident, now little more than a *smudge* in the air. "I'll be back as soon as I can. If I'm going to stop that thing, I'll need some kind of help."

"You pity me."

"I pity anyone who's not me, Fuzz. A hazard of being the man I am. But you *can* do this. Keep an eye on Ruin, and try to get word to Vin and that nobleman of hers."

"Pity," Preservation repeated. "Is that . . . is that what I've become? Yes . . . Yes, it is."

He reached up with a vaguely outlined hand and seized Kelsier's arm from underneath. Kelsier gasped, then cut off as Preservation grabbed him by the back of the neck with his other hand, locking his gaze with Kelsier's. Those eyes snapped into focus, fuzziness becoming suddenly distinct. A glow burst from them, silvery white, bathing Kelsier and blinding him.

Everything else was vaporized; nothing could withstand that terrible, wonderful light. Kelsier lost form, thought, very being. He transcended *self* and entered a place of flowing light. Ribbons of it exploded from him, and though he tried to scream, he had no voice.

Time didn't pass; time had no relevance here. It was not a place. Location had no relevance. Only Connection, person to person, man to world, Kelsier to god.

And that god was *everything.* The thing he had pitied was the very ground Kelsier walked upon, the air, the metals—his own soul. Preservation *was* everywhere. Beside it, Kelsier was insignificant. An afterthought.

The vision faded. Kelsier stumbled away from Preservation, who stood, placid, a blur in the air—but a representation of so much more. Kelsier put his hand to his chest and was pleased, for a reason he couldn't explain, to find that his heart was beating. His soul was learning to imitate a body, and somehow having a racing heart was comforting.

"I suppose I deserved that," Kelsier said. "Be careful how you use those visions, Fuzz. Reality isn't particularly healthy for a man's ego."

"I would call it very healthy," Preservation replied.

"I saw everything," Kelsier mumbled. "Everyone, everything. My Connection to them, and . . . and . . ."

Spreading into the future, he thought, grasping at

an explanation. *Possibilities, so many possibilities ... like atium.*

"Yes," Preservation said, sounding exhausted. "It can be trying to recognize one's true place in things. Few can handle the—"

"Send me back," Kelsier said, scrambling up to Preservation, taking him by the arms.

"What?"

"*Send me back.* I need to see that again."

"Your mind is too fragile. It will break."

"I broke that damn thing years ago, Fuzz. Do it. Please."

Preservation hesitantly gripped him, and this time his eyes took longer to start glowing. They flashed, his form trembling, and for a moment Kelsier thought the god would dissipate entirely.

Then the glow spurted to life, and in an instant Kelsier was consumed. This time he forced himself to look away from Preservation—though it was less a matter of *looking,* and more a matter of trying to sort through the horrible overload of information and sensation that assaulted him.

Unfortunately, in turning his attention away from Preservation he risked giving it to something else— something equally demanding. There was a second god here, black and terrible, the thing with the spines and spidery legs, sprouting from dark mists and reaching into everything throughout the land.

Including Kelsier.

In fact, his ties to Preservation were trivial by comparison to these hundreds of black fingers which attached him to that thing Beyond. He sensed a powerful satisfaction from it, along with an idea. Not words, just an undeniable fact.

You are mine, Survivor.

Kelsier rebelled at the thought, but in this place of perfect light, truth *had* to be acknowledged.

Straining, soul crumbling before that terrible reality, Kelsier turned toward the tendrils of light spreading into the distance. Possibilities upon possibilities, compounded upon one another. Infinite, overwhelming. The future.

He dropped out of the vision again, and this time fell to his knees panting. The glow faded, and he was again on the banks of Lake Luthadel. Preservation settled down beside him and rested his hand on Kelsier's back.

"I can't stop him," Kelsier whispered.

"I know," Preservation said.

"I could see thousands upon thousands of possibilities. In none of them did I defeat that thing."

"The ribbons of the future are never as useful as . . . as they should be," Preservation said. "I rode them much, in the past. It's too hard to see what is actually likely, and what is just a fragile . . . fragile, distant maybe. . . ."

"I can't stop it," Kelsier whispered. "I'm too like it. Everything I do serves *it*." Kelsier looked up, smiling.

"It broke you," Preservation said.

"No, Fuzz." Kelsier laughed, standing. "No. I can't stop it. No matter what I do, I can't stop it." He looked down at Preservation. "But *she* can."

"He knows this. You were right. He *has* been preparing her, infusing her."

"She can beat it."

"A frail possibility," Preservation said. "A false promise."

"No," Kelsier said softly. "A *hope*."

He held his hand out. Preservation took it and let Kelsier pull him to his feet. God nodded. "A hope. What is our plan?"

"I continue to the west," Kelsier said. "I saw, in the possibilities . . ."

"Do not trust what you saw," Preservation said, sounding far more firm than he had earlier. "It takes an infinite mind to even *begin* to glean information from those tendrils of the future. Even then you are likely to be wrong."

"The path I saw started by me going to the west," Kelsier said. "It's all I can think to do. Unless you have a better suggestion."

Preservation shook his head.

"You need to stay here, fight him off, resist—and try to get through to Vin. If not her, then Sazed."

"He . . . is not well."

Kelsier cocked his head. "Hurt in the fighting?"

"Worse. Ruin tries to break him."

Damn. But what could he do, except continue with his plan? "Do what you can," Kelsier said. "I'll seek these people to the west."

"They *won't* help."

"I'm not going to ask for their help," Kelsier said, then smiled. "I'm going to rob them."

PART FOUR
JOURNEY

1

Kelsier ran. He needed the urgency, the strength, of being in motion. A man running somewhere had a purpose.

He left the region around Luthadel, jogging alongside a canal for direction. Like the lake, the canal was reversed here—a long, narrow mound rather than a trough.

As he moved, Kelsier tried yet again to sort through the conflicting set of images, impressions, and ideas he'd experienced in that place where he could perceive everything. Vin *could* beat this thing. Of that Kelsier was certain, as certain as he was that he couldn't defeat Ruin himself.

From there however, his thoughts grew more vague. These people, the Ire, were working on something dangerous. Something he could use against Ruin . . . maybe.

That was all he had. Preservation was right; the threads in that place between moments were too knotted, too ephemeral, to give him much beyond a vague impression. But at least it was something he could do.

So he ran. He didn't have time to walk. He wished again for Allomancy, pewter to lend him strength and endurance. He'd had that power for such a short time, compared to the rest of his life, but it had become second nature to him very quickly.

He no longer had those abilities to lean on. Fortunately, without a body he did not seem to tire unless he stopped to think about the fact that he *should* be tiring. That was no problem. If there was one thing Kelsier was good at, it was lying to himself.

Hopefully Vin would be able to hold out long enough to save them all. It was a terrible weight to put on the shoulders of one person. He would lift what portion he could.

2

I know this place, Kelsier thought, slowing his jog as he passed through a small canalside town. A way-stop where canalmasters could rest their skaa, have a drink, and enjoy a warm bath for the night. It was one of many that dotted the dominances, all nearly identical. This one could be distinguished by the two crumbling towers on the opposite bank of the canal.

Yes, Kelsier thought, stopping on the street. Those towers were distinctive even in the dreamy, misted landscape of this Realm. Longsfollow. How could he have reached this place already? It was well outside the Central Dominance. How long had he been running?

Time had become a strange thing to him since his death. He had no need for food, and didn't feel tiredness beyond what his mind projected. With Ruin obstructing the sun, and the only light that of the misty ground, it was very difficult to judge the passing of days.

He'd been running . . . for a while. A long while?

He suddenly felt exhausted, his mind numbing, as if suffering the effects of a pewter drag. He groaned and sat down by the side of the canal mound, which was covered in tiny plants. Those plants seemed to grow anywhere water was present in the real world. He'd found them sprouting from misty cups.

Occasionally he'd found other, stranger plants in the landscape between towns—places where the springy ground grew more firm. Places without people: the extended, ashen emptiness between dots of civilization.

He heaved himself to his feet, fighting off the exhaustion. It was all in his head, quite literally. Reluctant to push himself back into a run for the moment, he strolled through Longsfollow. A town had grown up here around the canal stop. Well, a village. Noblemen who ran plantations farther out from the canal would come here to trade and to ship goods in toward Luthadel. It had become a hub of commerce, a bustling civic center.

Kelsier had killed seven men here.

Or had it been eight? He strolled, counting them off. The lord, both of his sons, his wife . . . Yes, seven, counting two guards and that cousin. That was right. He'd spared the cousin's wife, who had been with child.

He and Mare had been renting a room above the general store, over there, pretending to be merchants from a minor noble house. He walked up the steps outside the building, stopping at the door. He rested his fingers on it and sensed it in the Physical Realm, familiar even after all this time.

We had plans! Mare had said as they furiously packed. *How could you do this?*

"They murdered a child, Mare," Kelsier whispered. "Sank her in the canal with stones tied to her feet. Because she spilled their tea. Because she spilled the *damn tea.*"

Oh, Kell, she'd said. *They kill people every day. It's terrible, but it's life. Are you going to bring retribution to* every *nobleman out there?*

"Yes," Kelsier whispered. He made a fist against the door. "I did it. I made the Lord Ruler himself pay, Mare."

And that boiling mass of writhing serpents in the sky . . . that had been the result. He'd seen the truth, in his moment between time with Preservation. The Lord Ruler would have prevented this doom for another thousand years.

Kill one man. Get vengeance, but cause how many more deaths? He and Mare had fled this village. He'd later learned that Inquisitors had come, torturing many of the people they'd known here, killing not a few in their search for answers.

Kill, and they killed in turn. Get revenge, and their vengeance returned tenfold.

You are mine, Survivor.

He gripped at the door handle, but couldn't do more than gain an impression of how it looked. He couldn't move it. Fortunately, he was able to push against the door and force himself through. He stumbled to a stop, and was shocked to see that the room was occupied. A solitary soul—glowing, so it was a person in the real world, not this one—lay on the cot in the corner.

He and Mare had left this place in a hurry, and had been forced to stash some of their possessions in a hole behind a stone in the hearth. Those were gone now; he'd pilfered them after Mare's death, following his escape from the Pits and his training with the strange old Allomancer named Gemmel.

He avoided the person and walked to the small hearth. When he'd returned for that hidden coin, he'd been on his way to Luthadel, his mind overflowing with grand plans and dangerous ideas. He'd retrieved the coin, but had found more than he intended. The pouch of coin, and beside it a journal of Mare's.

"If I'd died," Kelsier said, loudly, "if I'd let myself be pulled into that other place . . . I'd be with Mare now, wouldn't I?"

No reply.

"Preservation!" Kelsier shouted. "Do you know where she is? Did you see her pass into that darkness you spoke of, in that place where people go after this? I'd be with her, wouldn't I, if I'd let myself die?"

Again Preservation didn't reply. His mind certainly wasn't in all places, even if his essence was. Considering how erratic he'd been lately, his mind might not be completely in even *one* place. Kelsier sighed, looking around the small room.

Then he stepped back, realizing that the person on the cot had stood up and was looking about.

"What do you want?" Kelsier snapped.

The figure jumped. Had he *heard* that?

Kelsier walked up to the figure and touched him, gaining a vision of an old beggar, scraggly of beard and wild of eye. The man was muttering to himself, and Kelsier—while touching him—could make some of it out.

"In me head," the man muttered. "Geddouta me head."

"You can hear me," Kelsier said.

The figure jumped again. "Damn whispers," he said. "Geddouta me head!"

Kelsier lowered his hand. He'd seen this, in the pulses. Sometimes the mad whispered the things they had heard from Ruin. But it seemed they could hear Kelsier as well.

Could he use this man? *Gemmel muttered like that sometimes,* Kelsier realized, feeling a chill. *I always thought he was mad.*

Kelsier tried to speak further with the man, but the effort was fruitless. The man kept jumping and muttering, but wouldn't actually respond.

Eventually Kelsier made his way back out of the room. He'd been glad for the madman to distract him from his memories of this place. He fished in his pocket, but then remembered he didn't have the picture of Mare's flower any longer. He'd left it for Vin.

He knew the answer to the questions he'd asked of Preservation just before. In refusing to accept death, Kelsier had also given up returning to Mare. Unless there was nothing beyond the warping. Unless *that* death was real and final.

Surely she couldn't have expected him to just give in, to let the stretching darkness take him? *Everyone else I've seen passed willingly,* Kelsier thought. *Even the Lord Ruler. Why must I insist on remaining?*

Foolish questions. Useless. He couldn't go when the world was in such danger. And he wouldn't just let himself die, not even to be with her.

He left the town, turned his path to the west again, and continued running.

3

Kelsier knelt down beside an old cookfire, no longer burning, represented by a group of shadowy, cold logs in this Realm. He found it was important to stop every few weeks or so to catch a breather. He had been running . . . well, a long time now.

Today he intended to finally crack a puzzle. He seized the misted remains of the old cookfire. Immediately he gained a vision of them in the real world—but he pushed through that, feeling something beyond.

Not just images, but sensations. Almost emotions. Cold wood that somehow remembered warmth. This fire was dead in the real world, but it *wished* it could burn again.

It was a strange sensation, realizing that logs could have wishes. This flame had burned for years, feeding the families of many skaa. Countless generations had sat before this pit in the floor. They'd kept the fire burning almost perpetually. Laughing, savoring their brief moments of joy.

The fire had given them that. It longed to do so again. Unfortunately, the people had left. Kelsier was finding more and more villages abandoned these days. Ashfalls went on longer than usual, and Kelsier had felt occasional trembling in the ground, even in this Realm. Earthquakes.

He could give this fire something. *Burn again,* he told it. *Be warm again.*

It couldn't happen in the Physical Realm, but all things there could manifest here. The fire wasn't actually alive, but to the people who had once lived here, it had been almost so. A familiar, warm friend.

Burn . . .

Light burst from his fingers, pouring out of his hands, a flame appearing there. Kelsier dropped it quickly, stepping back, grinning at the crackling blaze. It looked very much like the fire that Nazh and Khriss had carried with them; the logs themselves had appeared on this side, with dancing flames.

Fire. He'd made *fire* in the world of the dead. *Not bad, Kell,* he thought, kneeling. After taking a deep breath, he pushed his hand into the fire and grabbed the center of the logs, then closed his fist, capturing the bit of mist that made up the essence of that cookfire. It all folded upon itself, vanishing.

He cupped the small handful of mist. He could feel it, like he could feel the ground beneath him. Springy, but real enough as long as he didn't push too hard. He tucked the soul of the cookfire away in his pocket, fairly certain it wouldn't burst alight unless he commanded it to do so.

He left the skaa hovel, stepping out into a plantation. He'd never been here before—this was farther west than he'd traveled with Gemmel. The plantations out here were made of odd rectangular buildings that were low and squat, but each had a large courtyard. He strolled out of this one, entering a street that ran among a dozen similar hovels.

All in all, skaa were better off out here than they were in the inner dominances. It was like saying that a man drowning in beer was better off than one drowning in acid.

Ash fell through the sky. Though he'd not been able to see it during his first days in this Realm, he'd learned to pick it out. It reflected like tiny curling bits of mist, almost invisible. Kelsier broke into a jog, and the ash streamed around him. Some passed through him, leaving him with the impression that *he* was ash. A burned-out husk, a corpse reduced to embers that drifted on the wind.

He passed far too much ash heaped up on the ground. It shouldn't be falling so heavily here. The ashmounts were distant; from what he'd learned in his travels, ash only fell once or twice a month out here. Or at least that was how it had been before Ruin's awakening. Some trees still lived here, shadowy, their souls manifesting as misty forms that glowed like the souls of men.

He approached people on the road who were making

westward, toward the coastal towns. Likely their noblemen had already fled that direction, terrified by the sudden increase of ash and the other signs of destruction. As Kelsier passed the people, he stretched out his hand, letting it brush against them and give him impressions of each one.

A young mother lamed by a broken foot, carrying her new baby close to her breast.

An old woman, strong, as old skaa needed to be. The weak were often left to die.

A young, freckled man in a fine shirt. He'd stolen that from the lord's manor, most likely.

Kelsier watched for signs of madness or raving. He'd confirmed that those types could often hear him, though it didn't always require obvious madness. Many seemed unable to make out his specific words, but instead heard him as phantom whispers. Impressions.

He picked up speed, leaving the townspeople behind. He could tell that this was a well-traveled area from the light of the mists beneath him. During his months running, he'd come to understand—and to an extent even accept—the Cognitive Realm. There was a certain freedom to being able to move unhindered through walls. To being able to peek in at the people and their lives.

But he was so lonely.

He tried not to think about it. He focused on his run and the challenge ahead. Because of the way time blended here, it didn't feel to him as if months had passed. Indeed, this experience was far preferable to his sanity-grating year trapped at the Well.

But he missed the people. Kelsier needed people, conversation, friends. Without them he felt dried out. What he wouldn't have given for Preservation, unhinged as he was, to appear and speak to him. Even that white-haired *Drifter* would have been a welcome break from the wasteland of mists.

He tried to find madmen so he could at least have *some* interaction with other living beings, no matter how meaningless.

At least I've gained something, Kelsier thought. A campfire in his pocket. When he got out of this, and he *would* get out of it, he'd certainly have stories to tell.

4

Kelsier, the Survivor of Death, finally crested one last hill and beheld an incredible sight spread before him. Land.

It rose from the edge of the mists, an ominous, dark expanse. It felt less alive than the shifting white-grey mists beneath him, but oh was it a welcome sight.

He let out a long, relieved sigh. These last few weeks had been increasingly difficult. The thought of more running had started to nauseate him, and the loneliness had him seeing phantoms in the shifting mists, hearing voices in the lifeless nothing all around.

He was a much different figure from the one who had left Luthadel. He planted his staff on the ground beside him—he'd recovered that from the body of a dead refugee in the real world and coaxed it to life, giving it a new home and a new master to serve. Same for the enveloping cloak he wore, frayed at the edges almost like a mistcloak.

The pack he carried was different; he'd taken that

from an abandoned store. No master had ever carried it. It considered its purpose to sit on a shelf and be admired. So far it had still made for a suitable companion.

Kelsier settled down, putting aside his staff and digging into his pack. He counted off his balls of mist, which he kept wrapped up tight in the pack. None had vanished this time; that was good. When an object was recovered—or worse, destroyed—in the Physical Realm, its Identity changed and the spirit would return to the location of its body.

Abandoned objects were best. Ones that had been owned for a long while, so they had a strong Identity, but that currently had nobody in the Physical Realm to care for them. He pulled out the ball of mist that was his campfire and unfolded it, bathing in its warmth. It was starting to fray, the logs pocked with misty holes. He could only guess that he'd carried it too far from its origin, and the distance was distressing it.

He pulled out another ball of mist, which unfolded in his hand, becoming a leather waterskin. He took a long drink. It didn't do him any real good; the water vanished soon after being poured out, and he didn't seem to need to drink.

He drank anyway. It felt good on his lips and throat, refreshing. It let him pretend to be alive.

He huddled on that hillside, overlooking the new frontier, sipping at phantom water beside the soul of a fire. His experience in the realm of gods, that moment between time, was a distant memory now . . . but, honestly, it had felt distant from the second he'd fallen out of it. The brilliant Connections and eternity-spanning revelations had immediately faded like mist before the morning sun.

He'd needed to reach this place. Beyond that . . . he had no idea. There were people out there, but how did he find them? And what did he do when he located them?

I need what they have, he thought, taking another pull on the waterskin. *But they won't give it to me.* He knew that for certain. But what was it they had? Knowledge? How could he con someone when he didn't even know if they'd speak his language?

"Fuzz?" Kelsier said, just as a test. "Preservation, you there?"

No reply. He sighed, packing away his waterskin. He glanced over his shoulder toward the direction he'd come from.

Then he scrambled to his feet, ripping his knife from the sheath at his side and spinning about, putting the fire between him and what stood there. The figure wore robes and had bright, flame-red hair. He bore a welcoming smile, but Kelsier could see spines beneath the surface of his skin. Pricking spider legs, thousands of them, pushing against the skin and causing it to pucker outward in erratic motions.

Ruin's puppet. The thing he'd seen the force construct and dangle toward Vin.

"Hello, Kelsier," Ruin said through the figure's lips. "My colleague is unavailable. But I will convey your requests, if you wish it of me."

"Stay back," Kelsier said, flourishing the knife, reaching by instinct for metals he could no longer burn. Damn, he missed that.

"Oh, Kelsier," Ruin said. "Stay back? I'm all around you—the air you pretend to breathe, the ground beneath your feet. I'm in that knife and in your very soul. How exactly am I to 'stay back'?"

"You can say what you wish," Kelsier said. "But you don't own me. I am *not* yours."

"Why do you resist so?" Ruin asked, strolling around the fire. Kelsier walked the other direction, keeping distance between himself and this creature.

"Oh, I don't know," Kelsier said. "Perhaps because you're an *evil force of destruction and pain.*"

Ruin pulled up, as if offended. "That was uncalled for!" He spread his hands. "Death is not evil, Kelsier. Death is necessary. Every clock must wind down, every day must end. Without *me* there is no life, and never could have been. Life is change, and I represent that change."

"And now you'll end it."

"It was a gift I gave," Ruin said, stretching out his hand toward Kelsier. "Life. Wondrous, *beautiful* life. The joy of a new child, the pride of a parent, the satisfaction of a job well done. These are from *me.*

"But it is done now, Kelsier. This planet is an elderly man, having lived his life in full, now wheezing his last breaths. It is not evil to give him the rest he demands. It's a *mercy*."

Kelsier looked at that hand, which undulated with the pinprick pressing of the spiders inside.

"But who am I talking to?" Ruin said with a sigh, pulling back his hand. "The man who would not accept his own end, even though his soul longed for it, even though his wife longed for him to join her in the Beyond. No, Kelsier. I do not anticipate you will see the necessity of an ending. So continue to think me evil, if you must."

"Would it hurt so much," Kelsier said, "to give us a little more time?"

Ruin laughed. "Ever the thief, looking for what you can get away with. No, a reprieve has been granted time and time again. I assume you have no message for me to deliver, then?"

"Sure," Kelsier said. "Tell Fuzz he's to take something long, hard, and sharp, then ram it up your backside for me."

"As if he could harm even me. You realize that if he were in control, nobody would age? Nobody would think or live? If he had his way you'd all be frozen in time, unable to act lest you harm one another."

"So you're killing him."

"As I said," Ruin replied with a grin. "A mercy. For

an old man well past his prime. But if all you plan to do is insult me, I must be going. It's a shame you'll be off on that island when the end comes. I assume you'd like to greet the others when they die."

"It can't be *that* close."

"It is, fortunately. But even if you could have done something to help, you're useless out here. A shame."

Sure, Kelsier thought. *And you came here to tell me that, rather than remaining quietly pleased that I was off being distracted by my quest.*

Kelsier recognized a hook when he saw one. Ruin wanted him to *believe* that the end was very near, that coming out here had been pointless.

Which meant it wasn't.

Preservation said he couldn't leave to go where I'm going, Kelsier thought. *And Ruin is similarly bound, at least until the world is destroyed.*

Maybe, for the first time in months, he'd be able to escape that squirming sky and the eyes of the destroyer. He saluted Ruin, tucked away his fire, then strode down the hill.

"Running, Kelsier?" Ruin said, appearing on the hillside with hands clasped as Kelsier passed him. "You cannot flee your fate. You are tied to this world, and to me."

Kelsier kept on walking, and Ruin appeared at the bottom of the hill, in the same pose.

"Those fools in the fortress won't be able to help you," Ruin noted. "I think that once this world reaches its end, I will pay them a visit. They've existed far too long past what is right."

Kelsier stopped at the edge of the new land of dark stone, like the lake that had become an island. This one was even larger. The ocean had become a continent.

"I will kill Vin while you're gone," Ruin whispered. "I will kill them all. Think about that, Kelsier, on your journey. When you come back, if there's anything left, I might have need of you. Thank you for all you've done on my behalf."

Kelsier stepped out onto the ocean continent, leaving Ruin behind on the shore. Kelsier could almost see the spindly threads of power that animated this puppet, providing a voice to the terrible force.

Damn. Its words were lies. He *knew* that.

They hurt anyway.

PART FIVE
IRE

1

He'd hoped to have the sun back once Ruin vanished from the sky, but after walking far enough out, he seemed to leave his world behind—and the sun with it. The sky here was nothing but empty blackness. Kelsier eventually managed to use some vines to strap his flagging cookfire to the end of his staff, which became an improvised torch.

It was a strange experience, hiking through the darkened landscape, holding a staff with an entire *campfire* on the top. But the logs didn't fall apart, and the thing wasn't nearly as heavy as it should have been. Not as hot either, particularly if—when bringing it out—he didn't make it manifest fully.

Plant life grew all around him, real to his touch and eyes, though of strange varieties, some with brownish-red fronds and others with wide palms. Many trees—a jungle of exotic plants.

There were some bits of mist in here. If he knelt by the ground and looked for them, he could find little glowing spirits. Fish, sea plants. They manifested here above the ground, though in the ocean on the other side they were probably down within the depths. Kelsier stood up, holding the soul of some kind of massive deep-sea creature—like a fish, only as large as a building—in his hand, feeling its ponderous strength.

That was surreal, but so was his life these days. He dropped the fish's soul and continued onward, hiking through waist-high plants with a blazing staff lighting the way.

As he got farther from the shore, he felt a tugging at his soul. A manifestation of his ties to the world he'd left behind. He knew, without having to experiment, that this tug would ultimately grow strong enough that he wouldn't be able to continue outward.

He could use that. The tugging was a tool that let him judge if he was getting farther from his world, or if he'd gotten turned around in the darkness. Navigation was otherwise next to impossible, now that he didn't have the canals and roadways to guide him.

By judging the pull on his soul, he kept himself pointed directly outward, away from his homeland. He wasn't completely certain that was where he'd find his goal, but it seemed like his best bet.

He hiked through the jungle for days, but then it started to dwindle. Eventually he reached a place where plants grew only in occasional patches. They were replaced with strange formations of rock, like glassy sculptures. The jagged things were often some ten feet or more tall. He didn't know what to make of those. He had stopped passing the souls of fish, and nothing seemed to be alive out here in either Realm.

The pull tugging him backward was growing laborious to fight. He was beginning to worry he'd have to turn around when, at long last, he spotted something new.

A light on the horizon.

2

Sneaking was a great deal easier when you didn't technically have a body.

Kelsier moved in silence, having dismissed his cloak and staff. He'd left his pack behind, and though there were a few plants out here, he could pass *through* them, not even rustling their leaves.

The lights ahead pulsed from a fortress crafted of white stone. It wasn't a city, but close enough for him. That light had an odd quality; it didn't burn or flicker like a flame. Some kind of limelight? He drew near and pulled up beside one of the odd rock formations that were common out here. It had hooked spikes drooping from it almost like branches.

The very walls of this fortress glowed faintly. Was that mist? It didn't seem to have the same hue to it; it was too blue. Keeping to the shadows of rock formations, Kelsier rounded the building toward a brighter light source at the back.

This turned out to be an enormous glowing cord

as thick as a large tree trunk. It pulsed with a slow, rhythmic power, and the light it gave off was the same shade as the walls—only far more brilliant. It seemed to be some kind of energy conduit, and ran off into the far distance, visible in the darkness for miles.

The cord passed into the fortress through a large gate in the back. As Kelsier crept closer, he found that little lines of energy were running across the stone of the wall. They branched smaller and smaller, like a glowing web of veins.

The fortress was tall, imposing, like a keep—but without the ornamentation. It didn't have a separate fortification around it, but its walls were steep and sheer. Guards moved atop the roof, and as one passed, Kelsier pushed himself down into the ground. He was able to sink into it completely, becoming nearly invisible, though that required grabbing hold of the ground and pulling himself downward until only the top of his head was visible.

The guards didn't notice him. He climbed back out of the ground and inched up to the base of the fortress wall. He pressed his hand against the glowing stone and was given the impression of a rocky wall far from here, in another place. An unfamiliar land with striking *green* plants. He gasped, pulling his hand away.

These weren't stones, but the spirits of stones—like his spirit of a fire. They had been brought here and constructed into a building. Suddenly he didn't feel quite so clever at having found himself a staff and a sack.

He touched the stone again, looking at that green landscape. That was what Mare had talked about, a land with an open blue sky. *Another planet,* he decided. *One that didn't suffer our fate.*

For the moment he ignored the image of that place, pushing his fingers through the spirit of the stone. Strangely, the stone resisted. Kelsier gritted his teeth and pushed harder. He managed to get his fingers to sink in about two inches, but couldn't make them go any farther.

It's that light, he thought. It pushed back on him. *Looks a little like the light of souls.*

Well, he couldn't slip through the wall. What now? He retreated into the shadows to consider. Should he try to sneak in one of the gates? He rounded the building, contemplating this for a short time, before suddenly feeling foolish. He hurried forward to the wall again and pressed his hand against the stones, sinking his fingers in a few inches. Then he reached up and did the same with the other hand.

Then he proceeded to scale the wall.

Though he missed Steelpushing, this method proved quite effective. He could grip the wall basically anywhere he wanted, and his form didn't have much weight. Climbing was easy, as long as he maintained his concentration. Those images of a land with green plants were very distracting. Not a speck of ash in sight.

A piece of him had always considered Mare's flower a fanciful story. And while the place looked strange, it also attracted him with its alien beauty. There was something about it that was incredibly inviting. Unfortunately, the wall kept trying to spit his fingers back out, and maintaining his grip took a great deal of attention. He continued moving; he could revel in that luxurious scene of green grass and pleasant hills another time.

One of the upper levels had a window big enough to get through, which was good. The guards on the keep's top would have been difficult to dodge. Kelsier slipped in the window, entering a long stone corridor lit by the spiderwebs of power coursing across the walls, floor, and ceiling.

The energy must keep the stones from evaporating, Kelsier thought. All the souls he'd brought with him had begun to deteriorate, but these stones were solid and unbroken. Those tiny lines of power were somehow sustaining the spirits of the stone, and perhaps as a side effect keeping people like Kelsier from passing through the walls.

He crept down the corridor. He wasn't sure what he was searching for, but he wouldn't have learned anything more by sitting outside and waiting.

The power coursing through this place kept giving him visions of another world—and, he realized with discomfort, the energy seemed to be permeating him. Mixing with his soul's own energy, which had already been touched by the power at the Well. In a few brief moments, he had started to think that place with the green plants looked *normal*.

He heard voices echoing in the hallway, speaking a strange language with a nasal tone. Prepared for this, Kelsier scrambled out a window and clung there, just outside.

A pair of guards hurried through the hallway beside him, and after they passed he peeked in to see that they were wearing long white-blue tabards, pikes at their shoulders. They had fair skin and looked like they could have been from one of the dominances— except for their strange language. They spoke energetically, and as the words washed across him Kelsier thought . . . He thought he could make some of it out.

Yes. They speak the language of open fields, of green plants. Of where these stones came from, and the source of this power . . .

". . . is pretty sure he saw something, sir," one guard was saying.

The words struck Kelsier strangely. On one hand he felt they *should* be indecipherable. On the other hand he instantly knew what they meant.

"How would a Threnodite have made it all the way here?" the other guard snapped. "It defies reason, I tell you."

They passed through the doors at the other end of the hall. Kelsier climbed back into the corridor, curious. Had a guard seen him outside then? This didn't seem like a general alarm, so if he had been spotted, the glimpse had been brief.

He debated fleeing, but decided to follow the guards instead. Though most new thieves tried to avoid guards during an infiltration, Kelsier's experience showed that you generally wanted to tail them— for they'd always stick close to the things that were most important.

He wasn't certain if they could harm him in any way, though he figured it would be best not to find out, so he stayed a good distance back from the guards. After curving through a few stone corridors, they reached a door and went in. Kelsier crept up, cracked it, and was rewarded by the sight of a larger chamber where a small group of guards were setting up a strange device. A large yellow gemstone the size of Kelsier's fist shone in the center, glowing even more brightly than the walls. That gem was surrounded by a lattice of golden metal holding it in place. All told, it was the size of a desk clock.

Kelsier leaned forward, hidden just outside the door. That gemstone . . . that had to be worth a *fortune*.

A different door into the room—one opposite him— slammed open, causing several guards to jump, then salute. The creature that entered seemed . . . well, mostly human. Wizened, dried up, the woman had puckered lips, a bald scalp, and strange silvery-dark skin. She glowed faintly with the same quiet blue-white light as the walls.

"What is this?" the creature snapped in the language of the green plants.

The guard captain saluted. "Probably just a false alarm, ancient one. Maod says he saw something outside."

"Looked like a figure, ancient one," another guard piped up. "Saw it myself. It tested at the wall, sinking its fingers into the stone, but was rebuffed. Then it retreated, and I lost sight of it in the darkness."

So he *had* been seen. Damn. At least they didn't seem to know he'd crept into the building.

"Well, well," the ancient creature said. "My foresight does not seem so foolish now, does it, Captain? The powers of Threnody wish to join the main stage. Engage the device."

Kelsier had an immediate sinking feeling. Whatever that device did, he suspected it would not go well for him. He turned to bolt down the corridor, making for one of the windows. Behind him, the powerful golden light of the gemstone faded.

Kelsier felt nothing.

"Well," the captain said from behind, voice echoing. "Nobody from Threnody within a day's march of here. Looks like a false alarm after all."

Kelsier hesitated in the empty corridor. Then, cautious, he crept back to peek into the room. The guards and the wizened creature all stood around the device, seeming displeased.

"I do not doubt your foresight, ancient one," the

guard captain continued. "But I *do* trust my forces on the Threnodite border. There are no shadows here."

"Perhaps," the creature said, resting her fingers on the gemstone. "Perhaps there was someone, but the guard was wrong about it being a Cognitive Shadow. Have the guards be on alert, and leave the device on just in case. This timing strikes me as too opportune to be coincidental. I must speak with the rest of the Ire."

As she said the word, this time Kelsier got a sense of its meaning in the language of the green plants. It meant "age," and he had a sudden impression of a strange symbol made from four dots and some lines that curved, like ripples in a river.

Kelsier shook his head, dispelling the vision. The creature was walking in Kelsier's direction. He scrambled away, barely reaching a window and climbing out as the creature pushed open the door and strode through the hallway.

New plan, Kelsier decided, hanging outside on the wall, feeling completely exposed. *Follow the weird lady giving orders.*

He let her get a distance ahead of him, then entered the corridor and followed silently. She rounded the outer corridor of the fortress before eventually reaching the end of it, where it stopped at a guarded door. She passed inside, and Kelsier thought for a moment, then climbed out another window.

He had to be careful; if the guards above weren't already keeping close watch on the walls, they soon would be. Unfortunately, he doubted he could get through that doorway without bringing every guard in the place down on him. Instead he climbed along the outside of the fortress until he reached the next window past the guarded door. This one was smaller than the others he'd gone through, more like an arrow slit than a true window. Fortunately, it looked into the room the strange woman had entered.

Inside, an entire group of the creatures sat in discussion. Kelsier pressed up against the slit of a window, peeking in, clinging precariously to the wall some fifty feet in the air. The beings all had that same silvery skin, though two were a shade darker than the rest. It was difficult to distinguish individuals among them; they were all so old, the men completely bald, the women nearly so. Each wore the same distinctive robe—white, with a hood that could be pulled up and silver embroidery around the cuffs.

Curiously, the light from the walls was dimmer in the room. The effect was particularly noticeable near where one of the creatures was sitting or standing. It was like . . . they themselves were drawing in the light.

He was at least able to pick out the woman from before, with her wizened lips and long fingers. Her robe had a thicker band of silver. "We must move up our timetable," she was saying to the others. "I do not believe this sighting was a coincidence."

"Bah," said a seated man who held a cup of glowing liquid. "You always jump at stories, Alonoe. Not every coincidence is a sign of someone drawing upon Fortune."

"And do you disagree that it is best to be careful?" Alonoe demanded. "We have come too far, worked too hard, to let the prize slip away now."

"Preservation's Vessel *has* nearly expired," another woman said. "Our window to strike is approaching."

"An entire Shard," Alonoe said. "Ours."

"And if that was an agent of Ruin the guards spotted?" asked the seated man. "If our plans have been discovered? The Vessel of Ruin could have his eyes upon us at this very moment."

Alonoe seemed disturbed by this, and she glanced upward as if to search the sky for the watching eyes of the Shard. She recovered, speaking firmly. "I will take the chance."

"We will draw his anger either way," another of the beings noted. "If one of us Ascends to Preservation, we will be safe. Only then."

Kelsier chewed on this as the creatures fell silent. *So someone else can take up the Shard. Fuzz is almost dead, but if someone were to seize his power as he died . . .*

But hadn't Preservation told Kelsier that such a thing was impossible? *You wouldn't be able to hold my power anyway,* Preservation had said. *You're not Connected enough to me.*

He'd seen that now firsthand, in the space between moments. Were these creatures somehow Connected enough to Preservation to take the power? Kelsier doubted it. So what was their plan?

"We move forward," the seated man said, looking to the others. One at a time, they nodded. "Devotion protect us. We move forward."

"You won't need Devotion, Elrao," Alonoe said. "You will have *me*."

Over my dead body, Kelsier thought. Or . . . well, something like that.

"The timetable is accelerated then," said Elrao, the man with the cup. He drank the glowing liquid, then stood. "To the vault?"

The others nodded. Together they left the room.

Kelsier waited until they were gone, then tried pushing himself through the window. It was too small for a person, but he wasn't completely a person any longer. He could meld a few inches with the stone, and with effort he was able to contort his shape and *squeeze* through the wide slit.

He finally tumbled into the room, shoulders popping into their previous shape. The experience left him with a splitting headache. He sat up, back to the wall, and waited for the pain to fade before standing to give this room a thorough ransacking.

He didn't come up with much. A few bottles of wine, a handful of gemstones left casually in one of the drawers. Both were real, not souls pulled through to this Realm.

The room had a door leading into the inner parts

of the fortress, and so—after peeking through—he slipped in. This next room looked more promising. It was a bedroom. He rifled through the drawers, discovering several robes like the ones the wizened people had been wearing. And then, in the small table by the hearth, the jackpot. A book of sketches filled with strange symbols like the one he had visualized. Symbols that he felt, vaguely, he could understand.

Yes . . . These were writing, though most of the pages were filled with terms he couldn't begin to comprehend, even once he began to be able to read the symbols themselves. Terms like "Adonalsium," "Connection," "Realmatic Theory."

The end pages, however, described the culmination of the notes and sketches. A kind of arcane device in the shape of a sphere. You could break it and absorb the power within, which would briefly Connect you to Preservation—like the lines he'd seen in the space between moments.

That was their plan. Travel to the location of Preservation's death, prime themselves with this device, and absorb his power—Ascending to take his place.

Bold. Exactly the kind of plan Kelsier admired. And now, he finally knew what he was going to steal from them.

3

Thievery was the most authentic form of flattery.

What could be more satisfying than knowing the things you possessed were intriguing, captivating, or valuable enough to provoke another man to risk everything to obtain them? This was Kelsier's purpose in life, to remind people of the value of the things they loved. By taking them away.

These days, he didn't care for the *little* thieveries. Yes, he'd pocketed the gemstones he'd found up above, but that was more out of pragmatism than anything else. Ever since the Pits of Hathsin, he hadn't been interested in stealing common possessions.

No, these days he stole something far greater. Kelsier stole dreams.

He crouched outside the fortress, hidden between two spires of twisting black rock. He now understood the purpose of creating such a powerful building, here at the reaches of Preservation and Ruin's dominion. That fortress protected a vault, and inside that vault lay an incredible opportunity. The seed that would make a person, under the right circumstances, into a god.

Getting to it would be nearly impossible. They'd have guards, locks, traps, and arcane devices he couldn't plan for or expect. Sneaking in and robbing that vault would test his skills to their utmost, and even then he was likely to fail.

He decided not to try.

That was the thing about big, defended vaults. You couldn't realistically leave most possessions in them forever. Eventually you had to use what you guarded— and that provided men such as Kelsier with an opportunity. And so he waited, prepared, and planned.

It took a week or so—counting days by judging the schedules of the guards—but at long last an expedition sallied forth from the keep. The grand procession of twenty people rode on horseback, holding aloft lanterns.

Horses, Kelsier thought, slipping through the darkness to keep pace with the procession. *Hadn't expected that.*

Well, they weren't moving terribly quickly even with the mounts. He was able to keep up with them easily, particularly since he didn't tire as he had when alive.

He counted five of the wizened ancients and a force of fifteen soldiers. Curiously, each of the ancients was dressed almost exactly the same, in their similar robes with hoods up and leather satchels over their shoulders, the same style of saddlebags on each horse.

Decoys, Kelsier decided. *If someone attacks, they can split up. Their enemy might not know which of them to follow.*

Kelsier could use that, particularly since he was relatively certain who carried the Connection device. Alonoe, the imperious woman who seemed to be in charge, wasn't the type to let power slip through her spindly fingertips. She intended to become Preservation; letting one of her colleagues carry the device would be too risky. What if they got ideas? What if they used it themselves?

No, she'd have the weapon on her somewhere. The only question was how to get it from her.

Kelsier gave it some time. Days of travel through the darkened landscape, keeping pace with the caravan while he planned.

There were three basic types of thievery. The first involved a knife to the throat and a whispered threat. The second involved pilfering in the night. And the third . . . well, that was Kelsier's favorite. It involved a tongue coated with zinc. Instead of a knife it used confusion, and instead of prowling it worked in the open.

The best kind of thievery left your target uncertain whether anything had happened at all. Getting away with the prize was all well and good, but it didn't mean much if the city guard came pounding on your door the next day. He'd rather escape with half as many boxings, but the confidence that his trickery wouldn't be discovered for weeks to come.

And the *real* trophy was to pull off a heist so clever, the target didn't ever discover you'd taken something from them.

Each "night" the caravan made camp in an anxious little cluster of bedrolls around a campfire much like the one in Kelsier's pack. The ancients got out jars of light, drinking and restoring the luminance to their skin. They didn't chat much; these people seemed less like friends and more like a group of noblemen who considered one another allies by necessity.

Soon after their meal each night, the ancients retired to their bedrolls. They set guards, but didn't sleep in tents. Why would you need a tent out here? There was no rain to keep off, and practically no wind to block. Just darkness, rustling plants, and a dead man.

Unfortunately, Kelsier couldn't figure out a way to get to the weapon. Alonoe slept with her satchel in her hands, watched over by two guards. Each morning she checked to make sure the weapon was still there. Kelsier managed to get a glimpse of it one morning, and saw the glowing light inside, making him reasonably certain her satchel wasn't a decoy.

Well, that would come. His first step was to sow a little misdirection. He waited for an appropriate night, then pushed himself down into the ground, sinking his essence beneath the surface. Then he pulled himself through the rock. It was like swimming through very thick liquid dirt.

He came up near where Alonoe had just settled down to sleep, and stuck only his lips out of the ground. *Dox would have had a fit of laughter seeing this,* Kelsier thought. Well, Kelsier was far too arrogant to worry about his pride.

"So," he whispered to Alonoe in her own language, "you presume to hold Preservation's power. You think you'll fare better than he did at resisting me?"

He then pulled himself down under the ground. It was black as night under there, but he could hear the thumping of feet and the cries of shock from what he'd said. He swam out a distance, then lifted an ear from the ground.

"It was Ruin!" Alonoe was saying. "I swear, it must have been his Vessel. Speaking to me."

"So he does know," said another of the ancient ones. Kelsier thought it was Elrao, the man who had challenged her back in the fortress.

"Your wards were supposed to prevent this!" Alonoe said. "You told me they'd stop him from sensing the device!"

"There are ways for him to know of us without having sensed the orb, Alonoe," another female said. "My art is exacting."

"How he found us is not the problem," Elrao said. "The question is why he hasn't destroyed us."

"Preservation's Vessel still lives," the other woman said, musing. "That might be preventing Ruin's direct interference."

"I don't like it," Elrao said. "I think we should turn back."

"We have committed," Alonoe replied. "We press forward. No quarreling."

The stir in the camp eventually quieted down and the ancient ones turned back to their bedrolls, though more of the guards stayed awake than usual. Kelsier smiled, then pushed himself over beside Alonoe's head again.

"How would you like to die, Alonoe?" he whispered to her, then ducked beneath the earth.

This time they didn't go back to sleep. The next day it was a bleary-eyed party that set off across the dark landscape. That night, Kelsier prodded them again. And again. He made the next week a hell for the group, whispering to different members, promising them terrible things. He was quite proud of the various ways he came up with to distract, frighten, and unnerve them. He didn't get a chance to grab Alonoe's satchel—if anything, they were more careful with it than they had been. He did manage to snatch one of the other ones while they were breaking down camp one morning. It was empty save for a fake glass orb.

Kelsier continued his campaign of discord, and by the time the group reached the jungle of strange trees their patience had unraveled. They snapped at one another and spent less time each morning or night resting. Half the party was convinced they should turn back, though Alonoe insisted that the fact that "Ruin" only *spoke* to them was proof he couldn't stop them. She pressed the increasingly divided group forward, into the trees.

Which was exactly where Kelsier wanted them. Staying ahead of the horses would be easy in this snarl of a jungle, where he could pass through foliage as if it weren't there. He slipped on ahead and set up a little surprise for the group, then came back to find them bickering again. Perfect.

He pushed himself into the center of one of the trees, keeping only his hand outside, tucked at the back, holding the knife that Nazh had given him. As the line of horses passed, he reached out and swiped one of the animals on the flank.

The creature let out a scream of pain, and chaos broke out in the line. The people near the front—their nerves taut from a week spent being tormented by Kelsier's whispers—gave their horses their heads. Soldiers shouted, warning they were under attack. Ancient ones urged their beasts in different directions, some collapsing as the animals tripped in the underbrush.

Kelsier darted through the jungle, catching up to those in the front. Alonoe had kept her horse mostly under control, but it was even darker in these trees than outside, and the lanterns jostled wildly as the animals moved. Kelsier dashed past Alonoe to a point ahead where he'd strung his cloak between two trees and lashed it in place with vines.

He climbed a tree and reached into the cloak as the front of the line—haggard and reduced in numbers—arrived. He'd lashed his fire inside the cloak, and he brought it alive as they neared. The result was a burning, cloaked figure, appearing suddenly in the air above the already frazzled group.

They screamed, calling that Ruin had found them, and split apart, running their horses in a chaotic jumble—some in one direction, some in another.

Kelsier dropped to the ground and slipped through the darkness, staying parallel to Alonoe and the guard who managed to remain with her. The woman soon caught her horse in a snarl of undergrowth. Perfect. Kelsier ducked away and recovered his stash of supplies, then threw on one of the robes he'd found in the fortress. He scrambled through the brush, the robe catching on things, until he was just close enough for Alonoe to see.

Then he stepped out where she could see him and called to her, waving his hand. Thinking she'd found a larger group of her people, she and her lone guard trotted their horses toward him. That, however, only served to draw them away from the rest of the group. Kelsier led her farther from the others, then ducked away into the darkness, losing her and leaving her and her guard isolated.

From there he scrambled through the dark underbrush toward the rest of the group, his phantom heart pounding.

This. He'd *missed* this.

The con. The excitement of playing people like flutes, twisting them about themselves, tying their minds in knots. He hurried through the forest, listening to the shouts of fright, the calls of soldiers to one another, the snorts and cries of the horses. The patch of dense vegetation had become demonic disharmony.

Nearby, one of the wizened men was gathering soldiers and his colleagues, calling for them to keep their heads, and started leading them back in the direction they'd come, perhaps to regroup with those who had been lost when the line first scattered.

Kelsier—still wearing the robe and holding his stolen satchel over his shoulder—lay down on the ground in their path, and waited until someone spotted him.

"There!" a guard said. "It's—"

Kelsier sank himself down into the ground, leaving the robe and satchel behind. The guard screamed at the sight of one of the ancients apparently *melting* to nothing.

Kelsier crept up out of the ground a short distance away as the group gathered around his robe and satchel. "She *disintegrated,* ancient one!" the guard said. "I watched it with my own eyes."

"That's one of Alonoe's robes," a woman whispered, hand pulled to her breast in shock.

Another of the ancients looked in the satchel. "Empty," he said. "Merciful Domi . . . What were we thinking?"

"Back," Elrao said. "Back! Everyone get your horses! We're leaving. Curse Alonoe and this idea of hers!"

They were gone in moments. Kelsier strolled through the forest, stepping up beside the discarded robe—which they'd left—listening to the main bulk of the expedition crash through the jungle in their haste to escape him.

He shook his head, then took a short walk through the underbrush to where Alonoe and her lone guard were now trying to follow the sounds of the main body. They were doing a pretty good job of it, all things considered.

When the ancient one wasn't looking, Kelsier grabbed the guard around the neck and hauled him into the darkness. The man thrashed, but Kelsier got him in a quick lock and hold, knocking the man out without too much trouble. He pulled the body back quietly, then returned to find the solitary ancient one standing with lantern in hand beside her horse, turning frantically.

The jungle had become eerily still. "Hello?" she called. "Elrao? Riina?"

Kelsier waited in shadow as the calls became more

and more frantic. Eventually the woman's voice gave out. She slumped down in the forest, exhausted.

"Leave it," Kelsier whispered.

She looked up, red-eyed, frightened. Ancient or not, she could obviously still feel fear. Her eyes darted to one side, then the other, but he was too well hidden for her to spot him.

"*Leave it,*" Kelsier repeated.

He didn't need to ask again. She nodded, trembling, then took off her satchel and opened it, dumping out a large glass orb. The light from it was brilliant, and Kelsier had to step back lest it reveal him. Yes, there was power in that orb, great power. It was filled with glowing liquid that was far purer, and far brighter, than what the ancients had been drinking.

Exhaustion evident in her every move, the woman went to climb back onto her horse.

"Walk," Kelsier commanded.

She looked toward the darkness, searching, but didn't see him. "I . . ." she said, then licked her wizened lips. "I could serve you, Vessel. I—"

"*Go,*" Kelsier ordered.

Wincing, she unhooked the saddlebags and—lethargically—threw them over her shoulder. He didn't stop her. She probably needed those jars of glowing liquid to survive, and he didn't want her dead. He just wanted her to be slower than her companions. Once she found them, they might compare stories and realize they'd been had.

Or perhaps not. Alonoe struck out into the jungle. Hopefully they'd all conclude that Ruin had indeed bested them. Kelsier waited until she was gone, then strolled over and picked up the large glass orb. It showed no discernible way of being opened, other than shattering it.

He held the glowing orb before him and shook it, gazing at the incredible, mesmerizing liquid light within.

That was the most fun he'd had in ages.

PART SIX
HERO

1

Kelsier ran across a broken world. The trouble had been apparent the moment he left the ocean, stepping back onto the misty ground that made up the Final Empire. Here he'd found the wreckage of a coastal city. Smashed buildings, shattered streets. The entire city seemed to have *slid* into the ocean, a fact he wasn't able to fully piece together until he stood above the town and noticed the shadowy remains of buildings sticking from the ocean island farther up the coast.

From there it only grew worse. Empty towns. Vast piles of ash, which manifested on this side as rolling hills that he ran across for a time before realizing what they were.

Several days into his run home, he passed a small village where a few glowing souls huddled together in a building. As he watched, horrified, the roof collapsed, dumping ash on them. Three glows winked out immediately, and the souls of three ashen skaa appeared in the Cognitive Realm, their strings to the physical world cut.

Preservation didn't appear to greet them.

Kelsier grabbed one of them, an aged woman who— as he took her hand—started and looked at him with wide eyes. "Lord Ruler!"

"No," Kelsier said. "But close. What is happening?"

She started to stretch away. Her companions had already vanished.

"It's ending . . ." she whispered. "All ending . . ."

And she was gone. Kelsier was left holding empty air, disturbed.

He started running again. He'd felt guilty leaving the horse behind in the forest, but surely the animal was better off there than it would have been here.

Was he too late? Was Preservation already dead?

He ran himself hard, the heft of the glass orb weighing down his pack. Perhaps it was the urgency, but his course became even more singleminded than it had been during his trip out. He didn't want to see the failing world, the death all around him. Compared to that the exhaustion of the run was preferable, and so he sought it, running himself ragged.

He traveled for days upon days. Weeks upon weeks. Never stopping, never looking. Until . . .

Kelsier.

He jolted to a halt on a field of windswept ash. He had the distinct impression of mist in the physical world. Glowing mist. *Power.* He could not see that here, but he could sense it all around him.

"Fuzz?" he said, raising a hand to his forehead. Had he imagined that voice?

Not that way, Kelsier, the voice said, sounding distant. But yes, it *was* Preservation. *We aren't... aren't... there....*

The crushing weight of fatigue hit Kelsier. Where was he? He spun about, looking for some kind of landmark, but those were difficult to find out here. The ash had buried the canals; a few weeks back he remembered swimming down through the ground to find them. Lately... he'd just been running....

"Where?" Kelsier demanded. "Fuzz?"

So... tired...

"I know," Kelsier whispered. "I know, Fuzz."

Fadrex. Come to Fadrex. You are close....

Fadrex City? Kelsier had been there before, in his youth. It was just south of...

There. Just barely visible in the Cognitive Realm, he made out the shadowy tip of Mount Morag in the distance. That direction was north.

He turned his back toward the ashmount and ran for everything he was worth. It seemed a brief eyeblink before he reached the city and was given a welcome, warming sight. Souls.

The city was alive. Guards in the towers and on the tall rock formations surrounding the city. People in the streets, sleeping in their beds, clogging the buildings with beautiful, shining light. Kelsier walked right through the city gates, entering a wonderful, radiant city where people still fought on.

In the warmth of that glow, he knew he was not too late.

Unfortunately, his was not the only attention focused here. He had resisted looking upward during his run, but he could not help but do so now, confronting the churning, boiling mass. Shapes like black snakes slithered across one another, stretching to the horizon in all directions. It was watching. It was here.

So where was Preservation? Kelsier walked through the city, basking in the presence of other souls, recovering from his extended run. He stopped at one street corner, then spotted something. A tiny line of light, like a very long piece of hair, near his feet. He knelt, picking at it, and found that it stretched all the way along the street—impossibly thin, glowing faintly, yet too strong for him to break.

"Fuzz?" Kelsier said, following the strand, finding where it connected to another—it seemed a lattice that spread through the whole city.

Yes. I . . . I'm trying. . . .

"Nice work."

I can't talk to them . . . Fuzz said. *I'm dying, Kelsier. . . .*

"Hang on," Kelsier said. "I've found something; it's here in my pack. I took it from those creatures you mentioned. The Eyree."

I do not sense anything, Fuzz said.

Kelsier hesitated. He didn't want to reveal the object to Ruin. Instead he picked up the thread, which had enough slack for him to slip it into the pack and press it against the orb.

"How about that?"

Ahh . . . Yes . . .

"Can this help you somehow?"

No, unfortunately.

Kelsier felt his heart sink further.

The power . . . the power is hers. . . . But Ruin has her, Kelsier. I can't . . . I can't give it. . . .

"Hers?" Kelsier asked. "Vin? Is she here?"

The thread vibrated in Kelsier's fingers like the string of an instrument. Waves came along it from one direction.

Kelsier followed them, noticing again how Preservation had covered this city with his essence. Perhaps he figured that if he was going to be strung out anyway, he should lie down like a protective blanket.

Preservation led him to a small city square clogged with glowing souls and bits of metal on the walls. They glowed so brightly, particularly in contrast to the darkness of his months out alone. Was one of these souls Vin?

No, they were beggars. He moved among them, feeling at their souls with his fingertips, catching glimpses of them in the other Realm. Huddled in the ash, coughing and shivering. The fallen men and women of the Final Empire, the people even the common skaa tended to dismiss. For all his grand plans, he hadn't made the lives of these people better, had he?

He stopped in place.

That last beggar, sitting against an old brick wall . . . there was something about him. Kelsier backed up, touching the beggar's soul again, seeing a vision of a man with hands and face wrapped in bandages, white hair sticking out from beneath. Stark white hair, a fact not quite hidden by the ash that had been rubbed into it.

Kelsier felt a sudden shock, a painful *spike* that ran up his fingers into his soul. He jumped back as the beggar glanced his direction.

"You!" Kelsier said. "Drifter!"

The beggar shifted in place, but then glanced another direction, searching the square.

"What are you doing here?" Kelsier demanded.

The glowing figure gave no response.

Kelsier whipped his hand back and forth, trying to shake out the pain. His fingers had actually gone *numb*. What had that been? And how had the white-haired Drifter managed to affect him in *this* Realm?

A small glowing figure landed on a rooftop nearby.

"Oh, *hell*," Kelsier said, looking from Vin to the Drifter. He responded immediately, throwing himself toward the wall of the building and climbing desperately up it to Vin's side. "Vin. Vin, stay *away* from that man."

Of course yelling was pointless. She couldn't hear him.

Still, Kelsier seized her by the shoulders, seeing her in the Physical Realm. When had she grown so confident, so knowing? Those shoulders of hers had once cringed, but now they gave her the posture of a woman fully in control. Those eyes that had once widened in wonder were now narrowed with keen perception. Her hair was longer, but her slight build somehow seemed far more *powerful* than it had when he'd first met her.

"Vin," Kelsier said. "Vin! Listen, please. That man is trouble. Don't approach him. Don't—"

Vin cocked her head, then leaped off the roof, *away* from the Drifter.

"Hell," Kelsier said. "Did she actually hear me?"

Or was it a coincidence? Kelsier leaped after Vin, tossing himself carelessly from the building. He didn't have Allomancy, but he was light, and could fall without getting hurt. He landed softly and sprinted across the springy ground, tailing Vin as best he could, running *through* buildings, ignoring walls, trying to stay close. She still got ahead of him.

Kelsier . . . Preservation's voice whispered at him.

Something thrummed through him, a familiar jolt of power, a warmth within. It reminded him of burning metals. Preservation's own essence, empowering him.

He ran faster, jumped farther. It wasn't true Allomancy, but instead was something more raw and primal. It surged through Kelsier, warming his soul, letting him reach Vin—who had stopped in the street before a large building. Soon after he reached her, she took off again down the street, but this time Kelsier managed to keep pace, barely.

And she knew he was there. He could sense it in the way she leaped, trying to shake a tail, or at least catch sight of one. She was good, but this was a game he'd been playing for decades before she was born.

She *could* sense him. Why? How?

She sped up and he followed, with difficulty. His motions were clumsy; he had Preservation pushing him along, but he didn't have the finesse of true Allomancy. He couldn't Push or Pull; he merely jumped, grabbing hold of the shadowed walls of buildings, then throwing himself off in prowling leaps.

Still, he grinned widely. He hadn't realized how much he had missed training with Vin in the mists, matching himself against another Mistborn, watching his protégé inch toward excellence. She was good now. Fantastic even. Remarkable at judging the force of each Push, at balancing her own weight against her anchors.

This was energy; this was excitement. Almost he forgot the troubles he faced. Almost this was enough. If he could dance the mists with Vin at night, then finding a way to recapture his life in the Physical Realm might not matter so much.

They hit an intersection and turned toward the city's

perimeter. Vin bounded ahead on lines of steel; Kelsier hit the ground, thrumming with Preservation's power, and prepared to jump.

Something descended around him. A blackness of shredding spikes, of spider-leg scratches in the air, of jet-black mist.

"Well," Ruin said from all sides. "Well, well. Kelsier? How did I not see you earlier?"

The power suffocated him, pushing him toward the ground. Ahead, a small figure bounded after Vin, created of black mist and pulsing with a similar rhythm to what Kelsier had displayed. A decoy of some sort.

Like he did before, Kelsier thought. *Imitating Fuzz to trick Vin.* He struggled, frustrated, against his bonds.

Preservation, in turn, whimpered like a child in Kelsier's mind, then withdrew from him. The warming power faded from within Kelsier. Remarkably, as the power dampened, so did Ruin's ability to hold Kelsier down. Ruin's strength became less oppressive, and Kelsier was able to struggle to his feet and push through the veil of sharp mists, stumbling onto the street.

"Where *have* you been?" Ruin asked. The power behind Kelsier condensed, forming into the shape of the man he'd seen before, with the red hair. The motions beneath the man's skin were more subdued this time.

"Here and there," Kelsier said, glancing after Vin. He'd never catch up to her now. "I thought I'd see the sights. Find out what death has to offer."

"Ah, very coy. Did you visit the Ire? And got turned away from them, I assume. Yes, I can guess at that. What I want to know is why you returned. I thought for certain you would flee. Your part in this is done; you did what I needed you to."

Kelsier set down his pack, hopefully keeping hidden the orb of light inside. He walked forward, strolling around Ruin's manifestation. "My part?"

"The Eleventh Metal," Ruin said, amused. "You think that was a coincidence? A story nobody else had heard of, a secret way to kill an immortal emperor? It fell right in your lap."

Kelsier took it in stride. He'd already figured that Gemmel had been touched by Ruin, that Kelsier himself had been a pawn of the creature. *But why could Vin hear me?* What was he missing? He looked after Vin again.

"Ah," Ruin said. "The child. You still think she's going to defeat me, do you? Even after she set me free?"

Kelsier spun toward Ruin. Damn. How much did the creature know? Ruin smiled and stepped up to Kelsier.

"Leave Vin alone," Kelsier hissed.

"Leave her alone? She's mine, Kelsier. Just as you are. I've known that child since the day of her birth, and have been preparing her for even longer."

Kelsier gritted his teeth.

"So cute," Ruin said. "You actually thought this was all your idea, didn't you? The fall of the Final Empire, the end of the Lord Ruler . . . recruiting Vin in the first place?"

"Ideas are never original," Kelsier said. "Only one thing is."

"And what is that?"

"Style," Kelsier said.

Then he punched Ruin across the face.

Or he tried to. Ruin evaporated as his fist drew close, and a copy of him formed beside Kelsier a moment later. "Ah, Kelsier," he said. "Was that wise?"

"No," Kelsier said. "It was merely thematic. Leave her alone, Ruin."

Ruin smiled at him in a pitying way, then a thousand spindly, needlelike black spikes shot from the creature's body, ripping through the robes that made up its clothing. They pierced Kelsier like spears, fraying his soul, bringing a blinding wave of pain.

He screamed, falling to his knees. It was like the stretching when he'd first entered this place, only *forced, intrusive.*

He dropped to the ground, spasming, his soul leaking curls of mist. The spikes were gone, as was Ruin. But of course the creature was never *truly* gone. It watched from that undulating sky, covering everything.

Nothing can be destroyed, Kelsier, Ruin's voice whispered, intruding directly into his mind. *That's something humans can't understand. All things merely change, break down, become something new . . . something perfect.*

Preservation and I, we're two sides of the same coin, really. For when I am done, he shall finally have his desired stillness, unchangingness. And there won't be anything, body or soul, to disturb it.

Kelsier breathed in and out, using familiar motions from when he'd been alive to calm himself. Finally he groaned and rolled to his knees.

"You deserved that," Preservation noted, his voice distant.

"Sure did," Kelsier said, stumbling to his feet. "It was worth trying anyway."

2

Over the next few days, Kelsier tried to replicate his success in getting Vin to listen to him. Unfortunately, Ruin was watching for him now. Each time Kelsier got close, Ruin interfered, surrounding him, holding him back. Choking him with black smoke and driving him away.

Ruin seemed amused to keep Kelsier around the periphery of Vin's camp outside Fadrex, and didn't drive him away. But anytime Kelsier tried to speak directly with her, Ruin punished him. Like a parent slapping a child's hand for getting too close to the flame.

It was infuriating, more so because of the way Ruin's words dug at him. Everything Kelsier had accomplished had merely been part of this *thing's* master plan to be freed. And the creature *did* have some kind of hold on Vin. It could appear to her, as reinforced by how it led her away from the camp one day, in a sudden motion that confused Kelsier.

He tried to follow, running after the phantom that

Ruin had made. It bounded like a Mistborn and Vin followed, obviously convinced that she'd discovered a spy. They left the camp behind entirely.

Kelsier slowed, feeling useless, standing on the misty ground outside the city and watching them vanish into the distance. She could sense that thing, and as long as it was here it overshadowed Kelsier. He'd never be able to speak with her.

Ruin's reason for leading Vin away soon manifested. Something launched an assault on Vin and Elend's army of koloss. Kelsier figured it out from the bustling of the camp, and was able to reach the scene faster than the people in the Physical Realm. It looked like siege equipment had been rolled out onto a ridge above where the koloss camped.

It rained down death upon the beasts. Kelsier couldn't do anything but watch as the sudden attack killed thousands of them. He couldn't feel any real regret when the koloss were destroyed, but it did seem a waste.

The koloss raged in frustration, unable to reach their enemy. Curiously, their souls started to appear in the Cognitive Realm.

And they were human.

Not koloss at all, but *people,* dressed in a variety of outfits. Many were skaa, but there were soldiers, merchants, and even nobility among them. Both male and female.

Kelsier gaped. He had never quite known what koloss were, but he had not expected this. Common people, made beasts somehow? He rushed among the dying souls as they faded.

"What happened to you," he demanded of one woman. "How did this happen to you?"

She regarded him with a bemused expression. "Where," she said, "where am I?"

In a moment she was gone. It seemed the transition was too much of a shock. The others showed similar confusion, holding out their hands as if surprised to find themselves human again—though not a few seemed relieved. Kelsier watched as thousands of these figures appeared, then faded away. It was a slaughter on the other side, stones crashing down all around. One passed right through Kelsier before rolling away, breaking bodies.

He could use this, but he would need something specific. Not a skaa peasant, or even a crafty lord. He needed someone who . . .

There.

He dashed through fading spirits and dodged between the glowing souls of creatures not yet dead, making for a particular spirit who had just appeared. Bald, with tattoos circling his eyes. An obligator. This man seemed less surprised by events, and more resigned. By the time Kelsier arrived, the lanky obligator was already starting to stretch away.

"How?" Kelsier demanded, counting on the obligator to understand more about the koloss. "How did this happen to you?"

"I don't know," the man said.

Kelsier felt his heart sink.

"The beasts," the man continued, "should have known better than to take an obligator! I was their keeper, and they did this to me? This world is ruined."

Should have known better? Kelsier clutched the obligator's shoulder as the man stretched toward nothingness. "How? Please, *how* is it done? Men become koloss?"

The obligator looked to him and, vanishing, said one word.

"Spikes."

Kelsier gaped again. Around him on the misty plain, souls blazed bright, flashed, and were dumped into this Realm—before finally fading to nothing. Like human bonfires being extinguished.

Spikes. Like Inquisitor spikes?

He walked to the slumped-over corpses of the dead and knelt, inspecting them. Yes, he could see it. Metal glowed on this side, and among those corpses were little spikes—like embers, small but glowing fiercely.

They were much harder to make out on the living koloss, because of the way the soul blazed, but it seemed to him that the spikes pierced into the soul. Was that the secret? He shouted at a pair of koloss, and they looked toward him, then glanced about, confused.

The spikes transform them, Kelsier thought, *like Inquisitors. Is that how they're controlled? Through piercings in the soul?*

What of madmen? Were their souls cracked open, allowing something similar? Troubled, he left the field and its dying, although the battle—or rather the slaughter—seemed to be ending.

Kelsier crossed the misty field outside Fadrex, then lingered out here alone, away from the souls of men until Vin returned, trailed by a shadow she didn't seem to know was there this time. She passed by, then disappeared into the camp.

Kelsier settled down near one of the little tendrils of Preservation, and touched it. "He has his fingers in everything, doesn't he, Fuzz?"

"Yes," Preservation said, his voice frail, tiny. "See."

Something appeared in Kelsier's mind, a sequence of images: Inquisitors listening with heads raised toward Ruin's voice. Vin in the creature's shadow. A man he didn't know sitting on a burning throne and watching Luthadel, a twisted smile on his lips.

Then, little Lestibournes. Spook wore a burned cloak that seemed too big for him, and Ruin crouched nearby, whispering with Kelsier's *own voice* into the poor lad's ear.

After him, Kelsier saw Marsh standing among falling ash, spiked eyes staring sightlessly across the landscape. He didn't seem to be moving; the ash was piling up on his shoulders and head.

Marsh . . . Seeing his brother like that made Kelsier sick. Kelsier's plan had required Marsh to join the obligators. He had deduced what must have happened next. Marsh's Allomancy had been noticed, as had the fervent way he lived his life.

Passion and care. Marsh had never been as capable as Kelsier. But he had always, *always* been a better man.

Preservation showed him dozens of others, mostly people in power leading their followers to doom, laughing and dancing as ash piled high and crops withered in the mists. Each one was a person either pierced by metal or influenced by people around them who were pierced by metal. He should have made the connection back at the Well of Ascension, when he'd seen in the pulses that Ruin could speak to Marsh and the other Inquisitors.

Metal. It was the key to everything.

"So much destruction," Kelsier whispered at the visions. "We can't survive this, can we? Even if we stop Ruin, we are doomed."

"No," Preservation said. "Not doomed. Remember . . . hope, Kelsier. You said, I . . . I . . . am . . ."

"I am hope," Kelsier whispered.

"I cannot save you. But we must trust."

"In what?"

"In the man I was. In the . . . the plan . . . The sign . . . and the Hero . . ."

"Vin. He has her, Fuzz."

"He doesn't know as much as he thinks," Preservation whispered. "That is his weakness. The . . . weakness . . . of all clever men . . ."

"Except me, of course."

Preservation had enough spark left to chuckle at that, which did Kelsier some good. He stood up, dusting off his clothing. Which was somewhat pointless, seeing as how there was no dust here—not to mention no actual clothing. "Come now, Fuzz, when have you known me to be wrong?"

"Well, there was—"

"Those don't count. I wasn't fully myself back then."

"And . . . when did you become . . . fully yourself?"

"Only just now," Kelsier said.

"You could . . . you could use that excuse . . . anytime. . . ."

"Now you're catching on, Fuzz." Kelsier put his hands on his hips. "We use the plan you set in motion when you were sane, eh? All right then. How can I help?"

"Help? I . . . I don't . . ."

"No, be decisive. Bold! A good crewleader is always sure of himself, even when he isn't. *Especially* when he isn't."

"That doesn't make . . . sense. . . ."

"I'm dead. I don't need to make sense anymore. Ideas? You're crewleader now."

". . . Me?"

"Sure. Your plan. You're in charge. I mean, you *are* a god. That should count for something, I suppose."

"Thank you for . . . finally . . . acknowledging that. . . ."

Kelsier deliberated, then set his pack on the ground. "You're sure this can't help? It builds links between people and gods. I'd think it could heal you or something."

"Oh, Kelsier," Preservation said. "I've told you that I am dead already. You cannot . . . save me. Save my . . . successor instead."

"Then I will give it to Vin. Would that help?"

"No. You must tell . . . her. You can reach . . . through the gaps in souls . . . when I cannot. Tell her that she must not trust . . . pierced by metal. You must free her to take . . . my power. All of it."

"Right," Kelsier said, tucking away the glass globe. "Free Vin. Easy."

He just had to find a way past Ruin.

3

So, Midge," Kelsier whispered to the dozing man. "You got that?"

"Mission . . ." the scruffy soldier mumbled. "Survivor . . ."

"You can't trust anyone pierced by metal," Kelsier said. "Tell her that. Those exact words. It's a mission for you from the Survivor."

The man snorted awake; he was supposed to have been on watch, and he stumbled to his feet as his replacement approached. Kelsier regarded the glowing beings, anxious. It had taken precious days—during which Ruin had kept him far from Vin—to search out someone in the army who was touched in the head, someone with that distinctive soul of madness.

It wasn't that they were broken, as he had once guessed. They were merely . . . open. This man, Midge, seemed perfect. He responded to Kelsier's words, but he wasn't so unhinged that the others ignored him.

Kelsier followed Midge eagerly through camp to

one of the cookfires, where Midge started chatting, animatedly, with the others there.

Tell them, Kelsier thought. *Spread the news through camp. Let Vin hear it.*

Midge continued speaking. Others stood up around the fire. They were listening! Kelsier touched Midge, trying to hear what he was saying. He couldn't make it out though, until a thread of Preservation touched him—then the words started to vibrate through his soul, faintly audible to his ears.

"That's right," Midge said. "He talked to me. Said I'm special. Said we shouldn't trust none of you. I'm holy, and you just ain't."

"What?" Kelsier snapped. "Midge, you *idiot.*"

It went downhill from there. Kelsier stepped back as men around the cookfire squabbled and started shoving one another, then began a full-on brawl. With a sigh, Kelsier settled down on the misty shadow of a boulder and watched several days' worth of work evaporate.

Someone laid a hand on his shoulder, and he glanced toward Ruin, who had appeared there.

"Careful," Kelsier said, "you'll get *you* on my shirt."

Ruin chuckled. "I was worried, leaving you alone, Kelsier. But it seems you've been serving me well in my absence." One of the brawlers punched Demoux right across the face, and Ruin winced. "Nice."

"Needs to follow through more," Kelsier mumbled. "You need to really commit to a punch."

Ruin smiled a deep, knowing, insufferable smile. *Hell,* Kelsier thought. *I hope that's not what I look like.*

"You must realize by now, Kelsier," Ruin said, "that anything you do, I will counter. Struggle serves only Ruin."

Elend Venture arrived on the scene, gliding on a Steelpush that Kelsier envied, looking properly regal. That boy had grown into more of a man than Kelsier had ever expected he would. Despite that stupid beard.

Kelsier frowned. "Where is Vin?"

"Hm?" Ruin said. "Oh, I have her."

"Where?" Kelsier demanded.

"Away. Where I can keep her in hand." He leaned toward Kelsier. "Good job wasting time on the madman." He vanished.

I absolutely hate that man, Kelsier thought. Ruin . . . he was no more impressive, deep down, than Preservation was. *Hell,* Kelsier thought, *I'm better at this god stuff than they are.* At least he had inspired people.

Including Midge and the rest of the brawlers, unfortunately. Kelsier stood up from the rock and finally acknowledged a fact he'd been wanting to avoid. He couldn't do anything here, not with Ruin so focused on Vin and Elend right now. Kelsier had to get to someone else. Sazed maybe? Or perhaps Marsh. If he could get through to his brother while Ruin was distracted . . .

He had to hope that the wards on that orb would shade him from the dark god's eyes, as they had when Kelsier had first arrived at Fadrex. He needed to leave this place, strike out, lose Ruin's interest and then try to contact Marsh or Spook, get them to relay a message to Vin.

It hurt him to leave her behind in Ruin's clutches, but there was nothing more he could do.

Kelsier left that very hour.

4

Kelsier was nowhere in particular when God finally died.

He couldn't place the location. No town nearby, at least not one that hadn't been buried in ash. He had intended to head toward Luthadel, but with all the landmarks covered over—and with no sun to guide him—he wasn't certain he'd been going the right direction.

The land trembled, the misty ground quivering. Kelsier pulled up short, looking at the sky, at first expecting that Ruin was causing this tremor.

Then he felt it. Perhaps it was the small Connection he had to Preservation from his time at the Well of Ascension. Or maybe it was the piece inside him that the god had placed, the piece inside them all. The light of the soul.

Whatever the reason, Kelsier felt the end like a long, drawn-out sigh. It sent a chill up his spine, and he scrambled to find a thread of Preservation. They had been all over the ground earlier in his trip, but now he found nothing.

"Fuzz!" he screamed. "Preservation!"

Kelsier . . . The voice vibrated through him. *Goodbye.*

"Hell, Fuzz," Kelsier said, searching the sky. "I'm sorry. I . . ." He swallowed.

Odd, the voice said. *After all these years appearing for others as they died, I never expected . . . that my own passing would be so cold and lonely. . . .*

"I'm here for you," Kelsier said.

No. You weren't. Kelsier, he's splitting my power. He's breaking it apart. It will be gone . . . Splintered. . . . He'll destroy it.

"Like hell he will," Kelsier said, dropping his pack. He reached inside, gripping the glowing orb filled with liquid.

It's not for you, Kelsier, Preservation said. *It's not yours. It belongs to another.*

"I'll get it to her," Kelsier said, taking up the sphere. He drew in a deep breath, then used Nazh's knife to smash the orb, spraying his arm and body with the glowing liquid.

Lines like threads burst out from him. Glowing, effulgent. Like the lines from burning steel or iron, except they pointed at everything.

Kelsier! Preservation said, his voice strengthening. *Do better than you have before! They called you their god, and you were casual with their faith! The hearts of men are NOT YOUR TOYS.*

"I . . ." Kelsier licked his lips. "I understand. My Lord."

Do better, Kelsier, Preservation commanded, his voice fading. *If the end comes, get them below ground. It might help. And remember . . . remember what I told you, so long ago. . . . Do what I cannot, Kelsier. . . .*

SURVIVE.

The word vibrated through him, and Kelsier gasped. He knew that feeling, remembered that exact command. He'd heard that voice in the Pits. Waking him, driving him forward.

Saving him.

Kelsier bowed his head as he felt Preservation fade, finally, and stretch into the darkness.

Then, full of borrowed light, Kelsier seized the threads spinning around him and *Pulled.* The power resisted. He didn't know why—he had only a rudimentary understanding of what he was doing. Why did the power attune to some people and not others?

Well, he'd Pulled on stubborn anchors before. He yanked with all his might, drawing the power toward him. It struggled, defying him almost like it was alive . . . until . . .

It broke, flooding into him.

And Kelsier, the Survivor of Death, Ascended.

With a cry of exultation, he felt the power flow through him, like Allomancy a hundred times over. A feverish, molten, burning energy that washed through his soul. He laughed, rising into the air, expanding, becoming everywhere and everything.

What is this? Ruin's voice demanded.

Kelsier found himself confronted by the opposing god, their forms extending into eternity—one the icy coolness of life frozen, unmoving; the other the scrabbling, crumbling, violent blackness of decay. Kelsier grinned as he felt utter and complete *shock* from Ruin.

"What was it," Kelsier asked, "that you said before? Anything I can do, you will counter? How about this?"

Ruin raged, power flaring in a cyclone of anger. The persona cracked apart, revealing the *thing,* the raw energy that had plotted and planned for so long, only to be stopped now. Kelsier's grin widened, and he imagined—with delight—the sensation of ripping apart this monster that had killed Preservation. This useless, outdated waste of energy. Crushing it would be so *satisfying.* He willed his boundless power to attack.

And nothing happened.

Preservation's power resisted him still. It shied away from his murderous intent, and push though he would, he couldn't make it hurt Ruin.

His enemy vibrated, quivering, and the shaking became a sound like laughter. The churning dark mists recovered, transforming back into the image of a deific man stretching through the sky. "Oh, Kelsier!" Ruin cried. "You think I mind what you have done? Why, I'd have chosen for *you* to take the power! It's perfect! You're merely an aspect of me, after all."

Kelsier gritted his teeth, then stretched forth

fingers made of rushing wind, as if to grab Ruin and *throttle* him.

The creature merely laughed louder. "You can barely control it," Ruin said. "Even assuming it could harm me, you couldn't accomplish such a task. Look at you, Kelsier! You haven't form or shape. You're not alive, you're an *idea*. A *memory* of a man holding the power will never be as potent as a real one with ties to all three Realms."

Ruin shoved him aside with ease, though Kelsier felt a *crackling* at the thing's touch. These powers reacted to one another like flame and water. That made Kelsier certain there *was* a way to use the power he held to destroy Ruin. If he could figure it out.

Ruin turned his attention from Kelsier, and so Kelsier took to trying to acquaint himself with the power. Unfortunately, each thing he tried was met with resistance—both from Ruin's energy and from the power of Preservation itself. He could see himself now, in the Spiritual Realm—and those black lines were still there, tying him to Ruin.

The power he held didn't like that at all. It tumbled inside him, churning, trying to break free. He could hold on, but he knew that if he let go, it would escape him and he would never be able to recapture it.

Still, it was grand to be more than just a spirit. He could see into the Physical Realm again, though metal continued to glow brightly to his eyes. It was a relief to be able to see something other than misty shadows and glowing souls.

He wished that view were more encouraging. Endless seas of ash. Very few cities, dug out like craters. Burning mountains that spewed not only ash, but lava and brimstone. The land had cracked, creating rifts.

He tried not to think of that, but of the people. He could feel them, like he felt the very crust and core of the planet. He easily found which ones had souls that were open to him, and eagerly he swung down in. Surely among these he could find one who could deliver a message to Vin.

Yet they didn't seem to be able to hear him, no matter how he whispered to them. It was frustrating and baffling. He held the powers of eternity. How could he have lost the ability he'd had before, the ability to communicate with his people?

Around him, Ruin laughed.

"You think your predecessor didn't try that?" Ruin asked. "Your power cannot leak through those cracks, Preservation. It tries too hard to shore them up, to protect them. Only *I* can widen cracks."

Whether his reasoning was correct or not, Kelsier couldn't tell. But he did confirm time and time again that madmen could no longer hear him.

However, now *he* could hear people.

Everyone, not just the mad. He could hear their thoughts like voices—their hopes, their worries, their terrors. If he focused too long on them, directed his attention to a city, the multitude of thoughts threatened to overwhelm him. It was a buzz, a rush, and he found it difficult to separate individuals from the mess.

Above it all—land, cities, ash—hung the mists. They coated everything, even in the daytime. While trapped entirely in the Cognitive Realm, he hadn't seen how pervasive they were.

That's power, he thought, gazing upon it. *My power. I should be able to hold that, manipulate it.*

He couldn't. That left Ruin far stronger than he was. Why had Preservation left the mists untouched like that? It was still part of him, of course, but it was like . . . like a diffused army, spread as scouts throughout the kingdom, rather than gathered for war.

Ruin wasn't so inhibited. Kelsier could see his power at work now, revealed in ways that had been too grand for him to recognize before Ascending. Ruin ripped open the tops of ashmounts, holding them pried apart, letting death spew forth. He touched koloss all across the empire, driving them to murderous frenzies. When they ran out of people to kill, he gleefully turned them against one another.

He had hold of multiple people in every remaining city. His machinations were incredible—complex, subtle. Kelsier couldn't even follow all the threads, but the result was obvious: chaos.

Kelsier could do nothing about it. He held unimaginable power, yet he was *still* impotent. But importantly, Ruin had to *act* to counter him.

That was an important revelation. He and Ruin were both everywhere; their souls were the very bones of the planet. But their attention . . . that could only be divided so far.

If Kelsier tried to change things where Ruin was focused, he always lost. When Kelsier tried to stop the ashmounts, Ruin's arms ripping them open were stronger than his trying to seal them. When he tried to bolster Vin's armies with a sense of encouragement, Ruin acted like a blockade, keeping him away.

In a desperate attempt, he made a push to approach Vin herself. He wasn't certain what he could do, but he wanted to try battering Ruin away—push himself, and see what he was capable of doing.

He threw everything he had into it, straining against Ruin—feeling the friction of their essences meeting as he drew nearer to Vin, who was locked in a room within the palace of Fadrex. His essence meeting Ruin's caused shocks through the land, trembles. An earthquake.

He was able to draw close. He could feel Vin's mind, hear her thoughts. She knew so little—like he had known so little when he'd begun this. She didn't know about Preservation.

The clashing pushed Kelsier's essence away, ripping Preservation back from him, exposing his core—like a grinning skull as the flesh was torn free. A soul lined with darkness, but which was *Connected* to Vin somehow. Tied to her by the inscrutable lines that made up the Spiritual Realm.

"Vin!" he shouted, in agony, straining. The fight between him and Ruin caused the earthquake to intensify, and Ruin exulted in that destruction. It weakened his attention for a brief moment.

"Vin!" Kelsier said, getting closer. "Another god, Vin! There's another force!"

Confusion. She didn't see. Something leaked from Kelsier, drawing toward her. And with a shock, Kelsier saw a terrible sight, something he'd never suspected. A glowing spot of metal in Vin's ear, so similar to the color of her brilliant soul that he had missed it until he'd gotten very close.

Vin was spiked.

"What's the first rule of Allomancy, Vin!" Kelsier screamed. "The first thing I taught you!"

Vin looked up. Had she *heard*?

"Spikes, Vin!" Kelsier began. "You can't trust—"

Ruin returned and shoved Kelsier with a fierce burst of power, interrupting him. To hold on longer would have meant letting Ruin rip the power of Preservation away from him completely, and so he let himself go.

Ruin shoved him out of the building, out of the city entirely. Their clash brought incredible pain to Kelsier, and he couldn't help bearing the impression that—divine though he was—he was *limping* as he left the city.

Ruin was too focused on this place. Too strong here. He had almost all of his attention pointed at Vin and this city of Fadrex. He was even bringing in Marsh.

Maybe . . .

Kelsier tried to get close to Marsh, focusing his attention on his brother. Those same lines were there as had been with Vin, lines of Connection linking Kelsier's soul to his brother. Perhaps he could get through to Marsh too.

Unfortunately, Ruin spotted this too easily, and Kelsier was too weakened—too sore—from the previous clash. Ruin rebuffed him with ease, but not before Kelsier heard something emanating from Marsh.

Remember yourself, Marsh's thoughts whispered. *Fight, Marsh, FIGHT. Remember who you are.*

Kelsier felt a swelling of pride as he fled from Ruin. Something within Marsh, something of his brother, had survived. However, there was nothing Kelsier could do to help now. Whatever Ruin wanted in Fadrex, Kelsier would have to let him have it. To confront Ruin here was impossible, for Ruin could best Kelsier in a direct confrontation.

Fortunately, Kelsier had made a career of knowing when to avoid a fair fight. The con was on, and when the house guard was alert, your best bet was to lie low for a while.

Ruin watched Fadrex so intently, it would leave chinks elsewhere.

5

Do better, Kelsier.

He watched and waited. He could be careful.

The hearts of men are not your toys.

He floated, becoming the mists, observing how Ruin moved his pieces. The Inquisitors were his primary hands. Ruin positioned them deliberately.

The weakness of all clever men.

An opening. Kelsier needed an opening.

Survive.

Ruin thought he was in control all across the Final Empire. So sure of himself. But there were holes. He was devoting less and less attention to the broken city of Urteau, with its empty canals and starving people. One of his threads revolved around a young man who wore cloth wrapping his eyes and a burned cloak on his back.

Yes, Ruin thought he had this city in hand.

But Kelsier . . . Kelsier *knew* that boy.

Kelsier focused his attention on Spook as the young man—overwhelmed and driven to the brink of madness—stumbled onto a stage before a crowd. Ruin had driven him to this point by wearing Kelsier's form. He was trying to make an Inquisitor of the boy, while at the same time setting up the city to burn in riots and bedlam.

But his actions in this city were like so many others. His attention was too divided, with his only real focus on Fadrex. He worked in Urteau, but didn't *prioritize* it. He'd already set his plans in motion: Ruin the hopes of this people, burn the city to the ground. All it required was for a confused boy to commit a murder.

Spook stood onstage, prepared to kill in front of the crowd. Kelsier drew his attention in like a puff of mist, careful, quiet. He was the pulsing of the boards beneath Spook's feet, he was the air being breathed, he was the flame and fire.

Ruin was here, raging, demanding that Spook murder. It wasn't the careful, smiling persona. This was a purer, rawer form of the power. This piece of him had little of Ruin's attention, and he hadn't brought his full power to bear.

It didn't notice Kelsier as he drew back from the power, exposing his own soul and drawing it close to Spook. Those lines were there, the lines of familiarity, family, and Connection. Strangely, they were even *stronger* for Spook than they'd been for Marsh and Vin. Why would that be?

Now, you must kill her, Ruin said to Spook.

Under that anger, Kelsier whispered to Spook's broken soul. *Hope.*

You want power, Spook? Ruin thundered. *You want to be a better Allomancer? Well, power must come from somewhere. It is never free. This woman is a Coinshot. Kill her, and you can have her ability. I will give it to you.*

Hope, Kelsier said.

Back and forth. *Kill.* Ruin sent impressions, words. *Murder, destroy. Ruin.*

Hope.

Spook reached for the metal at his chest.

No! Ruin shouted, sounding shocked. *Spook, do you want to go back to being normal? Do you want to be useless again? You'll lose your pewter and go back to being weak, like you were when you let your uncle die!*

Spook looked at Ruin, grimaced, then cut into his body and pulled the spike free.

Hope.

Ruin screamed in denial, his figure fuzzing, spider-leg knives spearing out of the broken shape he wore. Destruction sprouted from the figure and became black mist.

Spook sank down onto the platform, slumping to his knees, then fell forward. Kelsier knelt and held him, drawing Preservation's power back to himself. "Oh, Spook," he whispered. "You poor, poor child."

He could feel the youth's spirit sputtering. *Broken.* Cracked through to the core. The boy's thoughts drifted to Kelsier. Thoughts of a woman he loved. Thoughts of his own failures. Confused thoughts.

Deep down, this boy had been following Ruin because he'd wished so desperately for Kelsier to guide him. He'd tried so hard to be like Kelsier himself.

It twisted Kelsier about, seeing the faith of this youth. Faith in him. Kelsier, the Survivor.

A pretend god.

"Spook," Kelsier whispered, touching Spook's soul with his own again. He choked on the words, but forced them out. "Spook, her city is burning."

Spook trembled.

"Thousands will die in the flames," Kelsier whispered. He touched the boy's cheek. "Spook, child. You want to be like me? Really like me? Then fight when you are beaten!"

Kelsier looked up at the spiraling, churning form of Ruin, angered. More of Ruin's attention was focusing in this direction. It would soon rebuff Kelsier.

Beating it here was only a small victory, but it was proof. This thing could be resisted. Spook had done it.

And would do it again.

Kelsier looked down at the child in his arms. No, not a child any longer. He opened himself to Spook, and spoke a single, all-powerful command.

"Survive!"

Spook screamed, burning his metal, startling himself to lucidity. Kelsier stood up, triumphant. Spook lurched to his knees, his spirit strengthening.

"Whatever you do," Ruin said to Kelsier, as if seeing him there for the first time, "I counter."

The force of destruction exploded outward, sending tendrils of darkness into the city. He didn't push Kelsier away. Kelsier wasn't certain if that was because his attention was still too focused elsewhere, or if he just didn't care whether Kelsier stayed to witness the end of this city.

Fires. Death. Kelsier saw the thing's plan in a flashing moment: Burn this city to the ground, extinguish all signs of Ruin's failure. End the people here.

Spook was already moving, confronting the people around him, giving orders as if he were the Lord Ruler himself. And was that . . .

Sazed!

Kelsier felt a comforting warmth upon seeing the quiet Terrisman stepping up to Spook. Sazed always had answers. But here he looked haggard, confused, *exhausted*.

"Oh, my friend," Kelsier whispered. "What has he done to you?"

The group obeyed Spook's orders, rushing off. Spook lagged behind them, walking down the street. Kelsier could see the threads of the future, in the Spiritual Realm. Coated in darkness, a city destroyed. Possibilities ending.

But a few lines of light remained. Yes, it was still possible. First this boy had to save his city.

"Spook," Kelsier said, forming himself a body of

power. Nobody could see him, but that didn't matter. He fell into step beside Spook, who practically stumbled along. One foot after the other, barely moving.

"Keep moving," Kelsier encouraged. He could feel this man's pain, his anguish and confusion. His faith battered. And somehow, through Connection, Kelsier could talk to him as he'd not been able to do to others.

Kelsier shared in Spook's exhaustion with each trembling, agonized step. He whispered the words over and over. *Keep moving.* It became a mantra. Spook's young woman arrived, helping him. Kelsier walked on his other side. *Keep moving.*

Blessedly, he did. Somehow the exhausted young man stumbled all the way to a burning building. He stopped outside, where Sazed had been forced to shy away. Kelsier read their attitudes in the slump of their shoulders, the fear in their eyes, reflecting flames. He heard their thoughts, pulsing from them, quiet and afraid.

This city was doomed, and they knew it.

Spook let the others pull him back from the fires. Emotions, memories, ideas rose from the boy.

Kelsier didn't care about me, Spook thought. *He didn't think of me. He remembered the others, but not me. Gave them jobs to do. I didn't matter to him. . . .*

"I named you, Spook," Kelsier whispered. "You were my friend. Isn't that enough?"

Spook stopped in place, pulling against the grip of the others.

"I'm sorry," Kelsier said, weeping, "for what you must do. Survivor."

Spook pulled from the grip of the others. And as Ruin raged above, sputtering and screaming—finally bringing in his attention to begin forcing Kelsier back—this young man entered the flames.

And saved the city.

6

Kelsier sat on a strange, verdant field. Green grass everywhere. So odd. So beautiful.

Spook walked over and settled down next to him. The boy removed the cloth from his eyes and shook his head, then ran his fingers through his hair. "What is this?"

"Half dream," Kelsier said, plucking a piece of grass and chewing on it.

"Half dream?" Spook asked.

"You're almost dead, kid," Kelsier said. "Smashed your spirit up pretty good. Lots of cracks." He smiled. "That let me in."

There was more to it. This young man was special. At the very least, their relationship was special. Spook believed in him as no other had.

Kelsier thought on this as he plucked another piece of grass and chewed on it.

"What are you doing?" Spook asked.

"It looks so strange," Kelsier said. "Like Mare always said it would."

"So you're *eating* it?"

"Chewing it, mostly," Kelsier said, then spat it to the side. "Just curious."

Spook puffed in and out. "Doesn't matter. None of this matters. You're not real."

"Well, that's partially right," Kelsier said. "I'm not completely real. Haven't been since I died. But then I'm also a god now . . . I think. It's complicated."

Spook looked at him, frowning.

"I needed someone I could chat with," Kelsier said. "I needed you. Someone who was broken, but who had resisted *him*."

"The other you."

Kelsier nodded.

"You always were so harsh, Kelsier," Spook said, staring out over the rolling green fields. "I could see that deep down, you *really* hated the nobility. I thought that hatred was why you were so strong."

"Strong like scar tissue," Kelsier whispered. "Functional, but stiff. It's a strength I'd rather you never need."

Spook nodded, and seemed to understand.

"I'm proud of you, kid," Kelsier said, giving him a fond punch to the arm.

"I almost ruined everything," he said, eyes downcast.

"Spook, if you knew how many times *I've* almost

destroyed a city, you'd be embarrassed to talk like that. Hell, you barely even broke that place. They've put out the fires, rescued most of the population. You're a hero."

Spook looked up, smiling.

"Here's the thing, kid," Kelsier said. "Vin doesn't know."

"Know what?"

"The spikes, Spook. I can't get the message to her. She needs to know. And Spook, she . . . she has a spike in her too."

"Lord Ruler . . ." Spook whispered. "Vin?"

Kelsier nodded. "Listen to me. You're going to wake soon. I need you to remember this part, even if you forget everything else about the dream. When the end comes, get people underground. Send a message to Vin. Scratch the message in metal, for anything not set in metal cannot be trusted.

"Vin needs to know about Ruin and his false faces. She needs to know about the spikes, that metal buried within a person lets Ruin whisper to them. Remember it, Spook. Don't trust anyone pierced by metal! Even the smallest bit can taint a man."

Spook began to fuzz, waking.

"Remember," Kelsier said. "Vin is hearing Ruin. She doesn't know who to trust, and that's why you absolutely must get that message sent, Spook. The pieces of this thing are all spinning about, cast to the wind.

You have a clue that nobody else does. Send it flying for me."

Spook nodded as he woke up.

"Good lad," Kelsier whispered, smiling. "You did well, Spook. I'm proud."

7

A man left Urteau, forging outward through the mists and the ash, starting the long trip toward Luthadel.

Kelsier didn't know this man, Goradel, personally. However, the power knew him. Knew how he'd joined the Lord Ruler's guards as a youth, hoping for a better life for himself and his family. This was a man whom Kelsier, if he'd been given the chance, would have killed without mercy.

Now Goradel might just save the world. Kelsier soared behind him, feeling the anticipation of the mists build. Goradel carried a metal plate bearing the secret.

Ruin rolled across the land like a shadow, dominating Kelsier. He laughed as he saw Goradel fighting through the ash, piled as high as snow in the mountains.

"Oh, Kelsier," Ruin said. "This is the best you can do? All that work with the child in Urteau, for this?"

Kelsier grunted as tendrils of Ruin's power sought out a pair of hands and brought them calling. In the real world hours passed, but to the eyes of gods time was a mutable thing. It flowed as you wished it to.

"Did you ever play card tricks, Ruin?" Kelsier asked. "Back when you were a common man?"

"I was never a common man," Ruin said. "I was but a Vessel awaiting my power."

"So what did that Vessel do with its time?" Kelsier asked. "Play card tricks?"

"Hardly," Ruin said. "I was a far better man than that."

Kelsier groaned as Ruin's hands eventually arrived, soaring high through the falling ash. A figure with spikes through his eyes, lips drawn back in a sneer.

"I was pretty good at card tricks," Kelsier said softly, "when I was a child. My first cons were with cards. Not three-card spin; that was too simple. I preferred the tricks where it was you, a deck of cards, and a mark who was watching your every move."

Below, Marsh struggled with—then finally slaughtered—the hapless Goradel. Kelsier winced as his brother didn't just murder, but reveled in the death, driven to madness by Ruin's taint. Strangely, Ruin worked to hold him *back*. As if in the moment, he'd lost control of Marsh.

Ruin was careful not to let Kelsier get too close. He couldn't even draw near enough to hear his brother's thoughts. Ruin laughed as, awash in the gore of the murder, Marsh finally retrieved the letter Spook had sent.

"You think," Ruin said, "you're so clever, Kelsier. Words in metal. I can't read them, but my minion can."

Kelsier sank down as Marsh felt at the plate Spook had ordered carved, reading the words out loud for Ruin to hear. Kelsier formed a body for himself and knelt in the ash, slumping forward, beaten.

Ruin formed beside him. "It's all right, Kelsier. This is the way things were *meant* to be. The reason they were created! Do not mourn the deaths that come to us; celebrate the lives that have passed."

He patted Kelsier, then evaporated. Marsh stumbled to his feet, ash sticking to the still-wet blood on his clothing and face. He then leaped after Ruin, following his master's call. The end was approaching quickly now.

Kelsier knelt by the corpse of the fallen man, who was slowly being covered in ash. Vin had spared him, and Kelsier had gotten him killed after all. He reached into the Cognitive Realm, where the man's spirit had stumbled in the place of mist and shadows, and was now looking skyward.

Kelsier approached and clasped the man's hand. "Thank you," he said. "And I'm sorry."

"I've failed," Goradel said as he stretched away.

It twisted Kelsier inside, but he didn't dare contradict the man. *Forgive me.*

Now, to be quiet. Kelsier let himself drift again, spread out. No longer did he try to stop Ruin's influence. In withdrawing, he saw that he *had* been helping a tiny bit. He'd held back some earthquakes, slowed the flow of lava. An insignificant amount, but at least he'd done something.

Now he let it go and gave Ruin free rein. The end accelerated, twisting about the motions of one young woman, who arrived back in Luthadel at the advent of a storm.

Kelsier closed his eyes, feeling the world hush, as if the land itself were holding its breath. Vin fought, danced, and pushed herself to the limits of her abilities—and then beyond. She stood against Ruin's assembled might of Inquisitors, and fought with such majesty that Kelsier was astonished. She was better than the Inquisitor he'd fought, better than any man he'd seen. Better than Kelsier himself.

Unfortunately, against an entire murder of Inquisitors, it was not nearly enough.

Kelsier forced himself to hold back. And *hell,* was it difficult. He let Ruin reign, let his Inquisitors beat Vin to submission. The fight was over too soon, and ended with Vin broken and defeated, at Marsh's mercy.

Ruin stepped close, whispering to her. *Where is the atium, Vin?* he said. *What do you know of it?*

Atium? Kelsier drew himself near as Marsh knelt by Vin and prepared to hurt her. Atium. Why . . .

It all came together for him. Ruin wasn't complete

either. There in the broken city of Luthadel—rain washing down, ash clogging the streets, Inquisitors roosting and watching with expressionless spiked eyes—Kelsier understood.

Preservation's plan. It could work!

Marsh snapped Vin's arm, and grinned.

Now.

Kelsier hit Ruin with the full strength of his power. It wasn't much, and he was a poor master of it. But it *was* unexpected, and it drew away Ruin's attention. The powers met, and the friction—the opposition—caused them to grind.

Pain coursed through Kelsier. The ground throughout the city trembled.

"Kelsier, Kelsier," Ruin said.

Below, Marsh laughed.

"Do you know," Kelsier said, "why I always won at card tricks, Ruin?"

"Please," Ruin said. "Does this matter?"

"It's because," Kelsier said, grunting in pain, his power taut, "I could always. Force. People to choose. The card *I wanted them to.*"

Ruin paused, then looked down. The letter—delivered by Goradel not to Vin, but to Marsh—did its job.

Marsh ripped free Vin's earring.

The world froze. Ruin, vast and immortal, looked on with complete and utter horror.

"You made the wrong one of us into your Inquisitor, Ruin," Kelsier hissed. "You shouldn't have picked the *good* brother. He always *did* have a nasty habit of doing what was right instead of what was smart."

Ruin looked to Kelsier, turning his full, incredible attention on him.

Kelsier smiled. Gods, it appeared, could still fall for a classic misdirection con.

Vin reached to the mists, and Kelsier felt the power within him tremble, eager. This was what they'd been meant for; this was their purpose. He felt Vin's yearning, and felt her question. Where had she felt this power before?

Kelsier rammed himself against Ruin, the powers clashing, exposing his soul. His darkened, battered soul.

"The power came from the Well of Ascension, of course," Kelsier said to Vin. "It's the same power, after all. Solid in the metal you fed to Elend. Liquid in the pool you burned. And vapor in the air, confined to night. Hiding you. Protecting you . . ."

Kelsier took a deep breath. He felt Preservation's energy being ripped from him. He felt Ruin's fury pummeling him, flaying him, ravenous to destroy him. For one last moment he felt the world. The farthest ashfall, the people in the distant south, the curling winds, and the life straining—struggling—to continue on this planet.

Then Kelsier did the most difficult thing he'd ever done.

"Giving you power!" he roared to Vin, letting go of Preservation's essence so she could take it up.

Vin drew in the mists.

And Ruin's full fury came against Kelsier, slamming him down, ripping into his soul. Tearing him apart.

8

Kelsier was cloven asunder with a rending, pervasive pain—like that of a bone being pulled from a socket. He tumbled, unable to see or think—unable to do more than scream at the attack.

He ended up someplace surrounded by mist, blind to anything beyond its shifting. Death, for real this time? No . . . but he was very close. He could feel the stretching coming upon him again, coaxing him, trying to pull him toward that distant point where everyone else had gone.

He wanted to go. He hurt *so much*. He wanted it all to end, to go away. Everything. He just wanted it to stop.

He had felt this despair before, in the Pits of Hathsin. He didn't have Preservation's voice to guide him now, as he had then, but—weeping, trembling— he sank his hands into the misty expanse around him and *held on*. Clinging to it, refusing to go. Denying that force that called to him, promising peace and an ending.

Eventually it stilled, and the stretching sensation faded away. He had held the power of deity. The final death could not take him unless he wanted it to.

Or unless he was completely destroyed. He shuddered in the mists, thankful for their embrace, but still uncertain where he was—and uncertain why Ruin hadn't finished the job. He'd planned to; Kelsier had felt that. Fortunately, Kelsier's destruction had become an afterthought in the face of a new threat.

Vin. She'd done it! She'd Ascended!

Groaning, Kelsier pulled himself upward, finding he'd been hit so hard by Ruin's attack that he'd been driven far down into the springy, misty ground of the Cognitive Realm. He was able to pull himself out, with difficulty, and collapsed onto the surface. His soul was distorted, mangled, like a body struck by a boulder. It leaked dark smoke from a thousand holes.

As he lay there it slowly re-formed, and the pain—at long last—faded. Time had passed. He didn't know how much, but it had been hours upon hours. He wasn't in Luthadel. De-Ascending—then being crushed by Ruin's power—had flung his soul far from the city.

He blinked phantom eyes. Above him the sky was a tempest of white and black tendrils, like clouds attacking one another. In the distance he could hear something that made the Realm tremble. He forced himself to his feet and walked, eventually cresting a hill where he saw—below—that figures made of light were locked in battle. A war, men against koloss.

Preservation's plan. He'd seen it, understood it in those last moments. Ruin's body was atium. The plan was to create something special and new—people who could *burn away* Ruin's body in an attempt to get rid of it.

Below, men fought for their lives, and he saw them transcending the Physical Realm because of the body of the god that they burned. Above, Ruin and Preservation clashed. Vin did a much better job of it than Kelsier had; she had the full power of the mists, and beyond that there was something *natural* about the way she held that power.

Kelsier dusted himself off and adjusted his clothing. Still the same shirt and trousers he'd been wearing during his fight with the Inquisitor long ago. What had happened to his pack and the knife Nazh had given him? Those were lost somewhere on the endless fields of ash between here and Fadrex.

He crossed through the battle, stepping out of the way of raging koloss and transcendent men who could see into the Spiritual Realm, if only in a very limited way.

Kelsier reached the top of a hill and stopped. On another hill beyond, distant but close enough to make out, Elend Venture stood among a pile of corpses, clashing with Marsh. Vin hovered above, expansive and incredible, a figure of glowing light and awesome power—like an inspiration for the sun and clouds.

Elend Venture raised his hand, and then *exploded* with light. Lines of white scattered from him in all directions, lines that drilled through all things. Lines that Connected him to Kelsier, to the future, and to the past.

He's seeing it fully, Kelsier thought. *That place between moments.*

Elend ended with a sword in Marsh's neck, and looked directly at Kelsier, transcending the three Realms.

Marsh slammed an axe into Elend's chest.

"No!" Kelsier screamed. "*No!*" He stumbled down the hillside, running for Venture. He climbed over corpses, shadowy on this side, and scrambled toward where Elend had died.

He hadn't reached the position yet when Marsh took off Elend's head.

Oh, Vin. I'm sorry.

Vin's full attention coursed around the fallen man. Kelsier pulled to a stop, numb. She would rage. She would lose control. She would . . .

Rise in glory?

He watched, awed, as Vin's strength coalesced. There was no hatred in the thrumming that washed from her, calming all things. Above her Ruin laughed, again assuming he knew so much. That laughter cut off as Vin rose against him, a glorious, radiant spear of power—controlled, loving, compassionate, but *unyielding*.

Kelsier knew then why she, and not he, had needed to do this.

Vin crashed her power against Ruin's, suffocating him. Kelsier stepped up to the top of the hill, watching, feeling a familiarity with that power. A kinship that warmed him deep within as Vin performed the ultimate act of heroism.

She brought destruction to the destroyer.

It ended in an eruption of light. Wisps of mist, both dark and white, streamed down from the sky. Kelsier smiled, knowing that at long last it was finished. In a rush, the mists swirled in twin columns, impossibly high. The powers had been released. They quivered, uncertain, like a storm brewing.

Nobody is holding them. . . .

Kelsier reached out, timid, trembling. He could . . .

Elend Venture's spirit stumbled into the Cognitive Realm beside him, tripping and collapsing to the ground. He groaned, and Kelsier grinned at him.

Elend blinked as Kelsier held out a hand. "I always imagined death," Elend said, letting Kelsier help him to his feet, "as being greeted by everyone I've ever loved in life. I hadn't imagined that would include *you*."

"You need to pay better attention, kid," Kelsier said, looking him over. "Nice uniform. Did you *ask* them to make you look like a cheap knockoff of the Lord Ruler, or was it more an accident?"

Elend blinked. "Wow. I hate you already."

"Give it time," Kelsier said, slapping him on the back. "For most that eventually fades to a sense of mild exasperation." He looked at the power still coursing around them, then frowned as a figure made of glowing light scrambled across the field. Its shape was familiar to him. It stepped up to Vin's corpse, which had fallen to the ground.

"Sazed," Kelsier whispered, then touched him. He was not prepared for the rush of emotion brought on by seeing his friend in this state. Sazed was frightened. Disbelieving. Crushed. Ruin was dead, but the world was still ending. Sazed had thought that Vin would save them. Honestly, so had Kelsier.

But it seemed there was yet another secret.

"It's him," Kelsier whispered. "He's the Hero."

Elend Venture placed a hand on Kelsier's shoulder. "You need to pay better attention," he noted. "Kid." He pulled Kelsier away as Sazed reached for the powers, one with each hand.

Kelsier stood in awe of the way they combined. He'd always seen these powers as opposites, yet as they swirled around Sazed it seemed that they actually *belonged* to one another. "How?" he whispered. "How is he Connected to them both, so evenly? Why not just Preservation?"

"He has changed, this last year," Elend said. "Ruin is more than death and destruction. It is peace with these things."

The transformation continued, but awesome though it was, Kelsier's attention was drawn by something else. A coalescing of power near him on the hilltop. It formed into the shape of a young woman who slipped easily into the Cognitive Realm. She didn't so much as stumble, which was both appropriate and horribly unfair.

Vin glanced at Kelsier and smiled. A welcoming, warm smile. A smile of joy and acceptance, which filled him with pride. How he wished he'd been able to find her earlier, when Mare was still alive. When she'd needed parents.

She went to Elend first, and seized him in a long embrace. Kelsier glanced at Sazed, who was expanding to become everything. Well, good for him. It was a tough job; Sazed could have it.

Elend nodded to Kelsier, and Vin walked over. "Kelsier," she said to him, "oh, Kelsier. You always did make your own rules."

Hesitant, he didn't embrace her. He reached out his hand, feeling oddly reverent. Vin took it, the tips of her fingers curling into his palm.

Nearby another figure had coalesced from the power, but Kelsier ignored him. He stepped closer to Vin. "I . . ." What did he say? Hell, he didn't know.

For once, he didn't know.

She embraced him, and he found himself weeping. The daughter he'd never had, the little child of the streets. Though she was still small, she'd outgrown him. And she loved him anyway. He held his daughter close against his own broken soul.

"You did it," he finally whispered. "What nobody else could have done. You gave yourself up."

"Well," she said, "I had such a good example, you see."

He pulled her tight and held her for a moment longer. Unfortunately, he eventually had to let go.

Ruin stood up nearby, blinking. Or . . . no, it wasn't Ruin any longer. It was just the Vessel, Ati. The man who had held the power. Ati ran his hand through his red hair, then looked about. "Vax?" he said, sounding confused.

"Excuse me," Kelsier said to Vin, then released her and trotted over to the red-haired man.

Whereupon he decked the man across the face, laying him out completely.

"Excellent," Kelsier said, shaking his hand. At his feet, the man looked at him, then closed his eyes and sighed, stretching away into eternity.

Kelsier walked back to the others, passing a figure in Terris robes standing with hands clasped before him, draping sleeves covering them. "Hey," Kelsier said, then looked at the sky and the glowing figure there. "Aren't you . . ."

"Part of me is," Sazed replied. He looked to Vin and Elend and held out his hands, one toward each of them. "Thank you both for this new beginning. I have healed your bodies. You can return to them, if you wish."

Vin looked to Elend. To Kelsier's horror, he had begun to stretch out. He turned toward something Kelsier couldn't see, something Beyond, and smiled, then stepped in that direction.

"I don't think it works that way, Saze," Vin said, then kissed him on the cheek. "Thank you." She turned, took Elend's hand, and began to stretch toward that unseen, distant point.

"Vin!" Kelsier cried, grabbing her other hand, clutching it. "No, Vin. You held the power. You don't have to go."

"I know," she said, looking back over her shoulder at him.

"Please," Kelsier said. "Don't go. Stay. With me."

"Ah, Kelsier," she said. "You have a lot to learn about love, don't you?"

"I know love, Vin. Everything I've done—the fall of the empire, the power I've given up—that was all *about* love."

She smiled. "Kelsier. You are a great man, and should be proud of what you've done. And you do love. I know you do. But at the same time, I don't think you understand it."

She turned her gaze toward Elend, who was vanishing, only his hand—in hers—still visible. "Thank you, Kelsier," she whispered, looking back at him, "for all you have done. Your sacrifice was amazing. But to do the things you had to do, to defend the world, you had to become something. Something that worries me.

"Once, you taught me an important lesson about friendship. I need to return that lesson. A last gift. You need to know, you need to ask. How much of what you've done was about love, and how much was about proving something? That you hadn't been betrayed, bested, beaten? Can you answer honestly, Kelsier?"

He met her eyes, and saw the implicit question.

How much was about us? it asked. *And how much was about you?*

"I don't know," he said to her.

She squeezed his hand and smiled—that smile she'd never have been able to give when he first found her.

That, more than anything, made him proud of her.

"Thank you," she whispered again.

Then she let go of his hand and followed Elend into the Beyond.

9

The land shook and groaned as it died, and was reborn.

Kelsier walked it, hands shoved in his pockets. He strolled through the end of the world, power spraying in all directions, giving him visions of all three Realms.

Fires burned from the heavens. Stones crashed together, then ripped back apart. Oceans boiled, and their steam became a new mist in the air.

Still Kelsier walked. He walked as if his feet could carry him from one world to the next, from one life to the next. He didn't feel abandoned, but he did feel alone. Like he was the only man left in all the world, and the last witness of eras.

Ash was consumed by a land of stones made liquid. Mountains crashed from the ground behind Kelsier, in rhythm to his footsteps. Rivers washed down from the heights and oceans filled. Life sprang up, trees sprouting and shooting toward the sky, making a forest around him. Then that passed, and he was in a desert, quickly drying, sand boiling from the depths of the land as Sazed created it.

A dozen different settings passed him in an eyeblink, the land growing in his wake, his shadow. Kelsier finally stopped on a lofty highland plateau overlooking a new world, winds from three Realms ruffling his clothing. Grass grew beneath his feet, then blossoms sprouted. Mare's flowers.

He knelt and bowed his head, resting his fingers on one of them.

Sazed appeared beside him. Slowly, Kelsier's vision of the real world faded, and he was trapped again in the Cognitive Realm. All became mist around him.

Sazed sat down next to him. "I will be honest, Kelsier. This is not the end I had in mind when I joined your crew."

"The rebellious Terrisman," Kelsier said. Though he was in the world of mist, he could see clouds—vaguely—in the real world. They passed beneath his feet, surging around the base of the mountain. "You were a living contradiction even then, Saze. I should have seen it."

"I can't bring them back," Sazed said softly. "Not yet . . . perhaps not ever. The Beyond is a place I can't reach."

"It's all right," Kelsier said. "Do me a favor. Will you see what you can do for Spook? His body is in rough shape. He's pushed it too hard. Fix him up a little?

Maybe make him Mistborn while you're at it. They're going to need some Allomancers in the world that comes."

"I'll consider it," Sazed said.

They sat there together. Two friends at the edge of the world, at the end and start of time. Eventually, Sazed stood and bowed to Kelsier. A reverent motion for one who was himself divine.

"What do you think, Saze?" Kelsier asked, staring out over the world. "Is there a way for me to get out of this, and live again in the Physical Realm?"

Sazed hesitated. "No. I do not think so." He patted Kelsier on the shoulder, then vanished.

Huh, Kelsier thought. *He holds the powers of creation in twain, a god among gods.*

And he's still a terrible liar.

EPILOGUE

Spook felt uncomfortable living in a mansion when everyone else had so little. But they had insisted—and besides, it wasn't much of a mansion. Yes, it was a log house of two stories, when most lived in shanties. And yes, he had his own room. But that room was small, and it felt muggy at night. They didn't have glass for windows, and if he left the shutters open, insects got in.

This perfect new world had a disappointing amount of normalcy to it.

He yawned, closing his door. The room held a cot and a desk. No candles or lamps; they didn't yet have the resources to spare those. His head was full of Breeze's instructions on how to be a king, and his arms hurt from training with Ham. Beldre would expect him for dinner shortly.

Downstairs a door thumped, and Spook jumped. He kept expecting loud noises to hurt his ears more than they did, and even after all these weeks he still wasn't used to walking around with his eyes uncovered. On his desk one of his aides had left a little writing board—they didn't have paper—scratched on with charcoal, listing a few of his appointments for the next day. And at the bottom was a quick note.

I finally got the smith to make this as you requested, though he was timid about handling Inquisitor spikes. Not sure why you want it so much, Your Majesty. But here you go.

At the base of the board was a tiny spike shaped like an earring. Hesitant, Spook picked it up and held it before him. Why *did* he want this, again? He remembered something, whispers in his dreams. *Get a spike forged, an earring. An old Inquisitor spike will work. You can find one in the caverns that used to be beneath Kredik Shaw. . . .*

A dream? He considered, then—perhaps against his better judgment—jabbed the thing through his ear.

Kelsier appeared in the room with him.

"Gah!" Spook said, leaping back. "You! You're dead. Vin killed you. Saze's book says—"

"It's okay, kid," Kelsier said. "I'm the real one."

"I . . ." Spook stammered. "It . . . Gah!"

Kelsier walked over and put his arm around Spook's shoulders. "See, I knew this would work. You've got them both now. Broken mind, Hemalurgic spike. You can see just enough into the Cognitive Realm. That means we can work together, you and I."

"Oh hell," Spook said.

"Now, don't be like that," Kelsier said. "Our work is important. *Vital*. We're going to unravel the mysteries of the universe. The cosmere, as it is called."

"What . . . what do you mean?"

Kelsier smiled.

"I think I'm going to be sick," Spook said.

"It's a big, big place out there, kid," Kelsier said. "Bigger than I ever knew. Ignorance almost lost us everything. I'm not going to let that happen again." He tapped at Spook's ear. "While dead, I had an opportunity. My mind expanded, and I learned some things. My focus wasn't on these spikes; I think I could have worked it all out, if it had been. I still learned enough to be dangerous, and the two of us are going to figure the rest out."

Spook pulled back. He was his own man now! He didn't need to just do whatever Kelsier said. Hell, he didn't even know if this really *was* Kelsier. He'd been fooled once before.

"Why?" Spook demanded. "Why would I care?"

Kelsier shrugged. "The Lord Ruler was immortal, you know. By a combination of the powers, he managed to make himself unable to age—unable to die, under most circumstances. You're Mistborn, Spook. Halfway there. Aren't you curious about what else is possible? I mean, we have a little pile of Inquisitor spikes, and nothing to do with them. . . ."

Immortal.

"And you?" Spook asked. "What do you get from this?"

"Nothing big," Kelsier said. "Just a little thing. Someone once explained my problem. My string has been cut, the thing holding me to the physical world." His smile broadened. "Well, we're just going to have to find me a new string."

POSTSCRIPT

I started planning this story while writing the original trilogy. By then, I'd pitched the idea of a "trilogy of trilogies" to my editor. (This is the idea that Mistborn, as a series, would change epochs and tech levels as the Cosmere matured.) I also knew that Kelsier would be playing a major role in future books in the series.

I'm not opposed to letting characters die; I believe that every series I've done has had some major, permanent casualties among viewpoint characters. At the same time, I was well aware that Kelsier's story was not finished. The person he was at the end of the first volume had learned some things, but hadn't completed his journey.

So, early on I began planning how to bring him back. I saturated *The Hero of Ages* with hints as to what he was doing behind the scenes, and even managed to slip in a few earlier hints here and there. I made very clear to fans who asked me that Kelsier was never good at doing what he was supposed to.

I am very aware of character resurrection as a dangerous trope, the balance of which I'm still figuring out. I didn't think this one was particularly controversial, in part because of the foreshadowing I'd done.

But I do want death to be a very real danger, or consequence, in my stories.

That said, Kelsier from the start was coming back— though at times I wavered on whether I was going to write this story or not. I was worried that if I wrote it out, it would feel disjointed, as so much time passes and so many different phases of storytelling had to occur. I started writing it a few years before I finally published it, tweaking scenes off and on, here and there.

Once I wrote *The Bands of Mourning,* it became clear to me that I'd need to get an explanation to readers out sooner rather than later. This set me to working on the story more diligently. In the end, I'm very pleased with how it turned out. It is a little disjointed, as I worried. However, the chance to finally talk about some of the behind-the-scenes stories going on in the Cosmere was very rewarding, both for myself and for fans.

To forestall questions, I do know what Kelsier and Spook were up to directly following this story. And I also know what Kelsier was doing during the era of the Wax and Wayne books. (There are some hints in those, as the original books have hints at this story.)

I can't promise that I'll write *Secret History 2* or *3.* There's already a lot on my plate. However, the possibility is in the back of my mind.

ABOUT THE AUTHOR

BRANDON SANDERSON grew up in Lincoln, Nebraska. He lives in Utah with his wife and children and teaches creative writing at Brigham Young University. He is the author of such bestsellers as the Mistborn* trilogy and its sequels, *The Alloy of Law, Shadows of Self,* and *The Bands of Mourning;* the Stormlight Archive* novels *The Way of Kings, Words of Radiance, Oathbringer,* and *Rhythm of War;* and young adult novels, including the Reckoners* series beginning with *Steelheart,* the Skyward series, *The Rithmatist,* and the Alcatraz vs. the Evil Librarians series. In 2013, he won a Hugo Award for Best Novella for *The Emperor's Soul,* set in the world of his acclaimed first novel, *Elantris.* Additionally, he was chosen to complete Robert Jordan's Wheel of Time® sequence. For behind-the-scenes information on all of Brandon Sanderson's books, visit brandonsanderson.com.